Disney

BEAUTY
AND THE
BEAST

D0826572

LOST IN A BOOK

JENNIFER DONNELLY

DISNEY PRESS
LOS ANGELES · NEW YORK

Copyright © 2017 Disney Enterprises, Inc.

All rights reserved. Published by Disney Press, an imprint of Disney Book Group. No part of this book may be reproduced or transmitted in any form or by any means, electronic or mechanical, including photocopying, recording, or by any information storage and retrieval system, without written permission from the publisher. For information address Disney Press, 1200 Grand Central Avenue, Glendale, California 91201.

Printed in the United States of America
First Hardcover Edition, January 2017
First Paperback Edition, September 2019

1 3 5 7 9 10 8 6 4 2

FAC-025438-19228
Library of Congress Control Number: 2016952932
ISBN 978-1-368-05768-4

Visit disneybooks.com

FOR EVERYONE WHO WANTS TO WRITE
THEIR OWN STORY

PROLOGUE

ONCE UPON FOREVER, in an ancient, crumbling palace, two sisters, Love and Death, played their eternal game.

Death was mistress of the palace, and any mortal who journeyed to its rusted gates never returned. Her face was as pale as a shroud, her hair as dark as midnight. She wore a black gown and a hunter's necklace of teeth, talons, and claws. Her emerald eyes narrowed as she contemplated the chessboard before her.

"It's your move," said Love.

"I'm quite aware of that," said Death.

"Tick-tock," said Love.

"Only fools rush Death," said Death.

Sighing, Love rose from the table where she and Death were seated. Her eyes were the same deep green as her sister's. Silvery blond hair tumbled down her back. Her dark skin was set off by a gown of white. Her only adornment was a necklace of twining willow branches. Shimmering beetles, bright butterflies, and dusky spiders clung to it, each a living jewel.

A tall mirror stood against a wall in the great hall where the sisters played, its silver frame mottled with tarnish. Love waved her hand over the glass and an image appeared. It showed a dining room—once grand, now ruined. Outside the room's mullioned windows, snow fell. Inside, a tormented creature—half-man, half-animal—paced. Back and forth he went, casting longing glances at the door. His eyes were fierce, but in their depths, haunted.

Death glanced up. "How *is* your beast these days?" she asked archly. "Still smashing furniture? Dinner plates? The windows?"

"I'm hopeful for him," Love replied, touching the glass. "For the first time."

"I don't know why," said Death. "Once a beast, always a beast."

"You always look for the worst in everyone," said Love reproachfully.

"And I always find it," Death said, her gaze directed at

the chessboard again. She frowned, drumming her crimson-tipped fingers on the table. Then, with a sly glance at her sister's back, she made her move.

"Poor little pawn. Such a pity," she drawled, nudging her knight across the board.

The china chess pieces were painted to resemble courtiers at a masquerade. The knight's face was hidden by an iron helmet. The pawn was costumed as a harlequin. Though fashioned of porcelain, they lived and breathed.

The knight advanced. The pawn raised her hands, begging for her life, but the knight, unmoved by her pleas, swung his sword and lopped off her head. China shards flew everywhere. The pretty head rolled across the board, its eyes still blinking.

Love turned around, startled by the sound of shattering porcelain. Her eyes flashed with anger as she viewed the board. "You *cheated*, Sister!" she exclaimed. "That knight was nowhere near my pawn!"

Death pressed a jeweled hand to her chest. "I certainly did *not*," she lied.

Love gave her a withering look. "It's my own fault," she said, sitting down again. "I should know better than to take my eyes off you, even for a second. You *hate* to lose."

Death leaned back in her chair, twining her fingers in her

necklace, trying not to smirk. As she waited for her sister to make a move, her eyes traveled around the room. Antlers hung above the stone mantel. The heads of boars and wolves adorned the walls, firelight dancing in their glass eyes.

A sudden movement in the mirror caught Death's attention. The glass now showed a magnificent library, and in it—a young woman. She was wearing the plain blue dress of a village girl. Her thick dark tresses were tied up with a ribbon, and her warm brown eyes sparkled with humor and intelligence.

Death's gaze sharpened at the appearance of the girl, like a lion's at the sight of a gazelle. "Belle," she whispered. "So beautiful, just like your name."

Love glanced at the mirror. "You know the girl?" she asked.

"I've known her for quite some time. She was a babe in her mother's arms when we met."

As Death watched, Belle pulled a book off a shelf, then held it up, smiling. The Beast squinted at it, trying to read the title. Belle opened the book and read the first page. Her head bent, she didn't see the sadness in the Beast's eyes turn to happiness.

Love, her fingers poised over the chessboard now, said, "That girl will be the one, mark my words. She's brave, stubborn—even more stubborn than the Beast is—and she has a heart of gold."

"Mmm, but it's not the *girl's* heart that's in question, is it?" Death mused.

Love, her brow furrowed in concentration, barely heard her sister. Nor did she notice as a horned beetle flew off her necklace and landed atop the mirror.

"It's the *Beast's* heart we're concerned with," Death continued. "Have you forgotten how he behaved when he was still a prince? Why, on the very day he was enchanted, he spent alms meant for the poor on a new carriage, made fun of a kitchen boy's stutter, and ran a stag to death with his hounds. I would have turned the fool into a worm and crushed him under my boot, but you did not. Why, I'll never know."

"Because he deserves a second chance," Love said. "Everyone does. My enchantress transformed the outer man to transform the inner. His suffering will teach him kindness and compassion. He'll find his heart again."

Death groaned in exasperation. "He *has* no heart, Sister! One cannot find that which never existed!"

Love's eyes, bright with feeling, met Death's. "You're wrong," she said. "I've watched him since he was a child. I saw what happened to him, how cruelly his father treated him. He had to hide his heart. It was the only way he could survive!"

Death waved a dismissive hand at her, but Love did not give up. Giving up was not in her nature. "Have you ever seen a bear made to fight off dogs in a village square for sport?" she asked. "Have you seen how it snarls and snaps? Pain, fear . . . they can turn you into something you were never meant to be. The Beast can change."

"He'd better be quick about it. That rose of yours looks none too healthy," Death said, nodding at the mirror.

It now showed a table in the Beast's castle. Candlelight fell upon it, illuminating a single red rose suspended in a glass cloche. The rose's head drooped. Withered petals lay under it. As Death and Love watched, another one dropped.

"If the Beast doesn't succeed in winning Belle's love by the time the last petal falls, he must remain a beast forever," said Death. "You took a gamble, dear sister, on the human heart—a fool's bet if ever there was one. Me? I'd wager a million louis d'or that the Beast fails."

Love raised an eyebrow. "One million gold coins? You must be rich indeed if you can afford to lose such a sum," she said, returning her attention to the chessboard.

Death smiled patronizingly. In a voice dripping with fake sympathy, she said, "I understand. You don't want to bet. It's too much money. You're afraid—"

"Of *nothing*. Least of all you," Love retorted. "Make it *two* million."

Death's eyes lit up. There was nothing she loved more than gambling. Just yesterday, she'd heard a young baroness on horseback say, "I bet I can jump that fence!" and a farm boy boast, "I bet I can swim across that river!" She'd won both of *those* wagers handily.

Love was the same way. The higher the stakes, the more impossible the odds, the more eager she was to up the ante. It was the one thing the two sisters had in common.

"That gold is as good as mine," Death said. "Humans are selfish creatures who can always be counted on to do the wrong thing. Shall I tell you how the story ends? The Beast is horrible to Belle, she abandons him, the last petal falls. *Fini.*"

Love jutted her chin. "You have no idea how the story ends. You're not its author. Sometimes kindness and gentleness win."

Death snorted. "And sometimes unicorns gallop down rainbows."

Love glared at her. "*Three* million."

"Done!" Death crowed. "I'm going to win the wager, Sister dearest. Just you wait and see."

"Well, you certainly didn't win this game," Love said, sliding her queen across the board. "Checkmate."

Death's smile slid off her face. She looked down at the board and saw Love's queen standing in front of her own king. *"What?"* she said, shocked. "It can't be!"

As Love and Death watched, the queen offered the king a kiss. Surprised by so sweet a mercy, the king embraced the queen. A second later, he crumpled to the board, a dagger sticking out of his back.

"And they say *I'm* ruthless!" Death exclaimed.

Smiling triumphantly, Love rose from her chair. She kissed her sister's cold cheek and said, "Don't get up. I'll see myself out."

Death sat perfectly still, glowering at the chess pieces. Her bishop looked up at her and started to shake. His knees knocked. A crack appeared on his painted face. Fuming, Death swept the pieces off the board. They shattered on the stone floor. Then she rose and walked to the mirror. Her expression, already sour, curdled as she watched the Beast and Belle—still enjoying their books, and each other's company.

The girl was frightened of him at first, Death thought, *and who wouldn't be? But she isn't anymore. This girl is the rarest of creatures— one who sees with her heart. My sister is right. She could be the one. And that won't do.*

Turning on her heel, her skirts swirling behind her like an ill wind, Death crossed the room to a towering cabinet. She opened it, then ran a finger over the books on its shelves.

"There you are!" she whispered, pulling one out.

Bound in black leather, the book was dusty and old. Its spine was cracked, but its title was still visible: NEVERMORE.

"Mouchard! Truqué!" Death barked. "Come!"

Two vultures left their roost atop the mantel and flew to her. They were enormous birds with coal-black feathers and cruel beaks. A dozen more just like them were perched around the room.

"Take this book to the Beast's castle. Put it in the library," Death commanded. "Be sure no one sees you."

One of the vultures let out a harsh squawk.

"No, Mouchard, you insolent creature, it's *not* cheating," Death said. "It's just stacking the deck a bit. You think my sister won't do the same? You know what she's like. She acts as if she's made of dewdrops and moonbeams, but she's ferocious. A sweet-faced little savage. She'll stop at nothing to win the wager."

The second vulture screeched. He shook his head, and then his wings. Death's pale cheeks flushed with indignation.

"I *know* there are rules, Truqué!" she said. "I *know* I cannot go to the girl before her time. But what if she comes to me?

What if I can bind her here? That changes things, doesn't it?"

The vulture considered his mistress's words, then dipped his head and grabbed the book with his sharp talons. Death opened a window, and the two birds swooped off into the night. As she watched them go, her sister's words came back to her.

You have no idea how the story ends.

Death's bloodred lips curved into a grim, determined smile.

"Oh, but I *do*," she purred. "Because *I* intend to write it."

CHAPTER ONE

BELLE STOOD IN FRONT of the doors to the library holding a mop in one hand, a bucket in the other, and wearing a wide, excited grin.

Arrayed on the floor around her were several objects—a gleaming golden candelabrum in the shape of a man, a stocky bronze mantel clock, a squat porcelain teapot, a little teacup with a chip in its rim, a feather duster with a peacock-shaped handle, and a four-legged fringed footstool.

The candelabrum spoke first.

"My darling girl, you're holding that mop as if it were a sword," he teased. "You look like you're going into battle!"

He had flaming candles instead of hands, and he flourished one dramatically now, as if challenging Belle to a duel.

"I *am* going into battle, Lumiere, and so are you. You have no idea what's waiting beyond those doors," Belle said, laughing.

Lumiere grimaced. "Actually, I do," he said. "The master has many admirable qualities, but tidiness is not one of them."

"Stuff and nonsense!" declared the mantel clock, pushing his way past them. "Are you forgetting that I rode with the comte de Rochambeau at the Siege of Yorktown?"

Lumiere rolled his eyes. "Not for a second, *mon ami*," he said.

"We trounced the redcoats and sent them packing! This old soldier is more than a match for a couple of cobwebs!" Cogsworth declared.

He gave the massive doors a push. They swung open, hinges groaning. As they did, Cogsworth, still blustering, fell silent. He took a few steps into the cavernous room. The other servants joined him. Everyone stared in horror at the scene before them. Everyone but Belle.

CHAPTER TWO

WITH A CRY OF DELIGHT, Belle ran into the center of the room, put her mop and bucket down, and turned around in a wide circle, her face full of wonder.

It seemed to her that every book ever written was here. There were novels and plays. Love poems. Legends and folktales. Volumes of philosophy, history, science, mathematics. Earlier that morning, when she'd first opened her eyes, she was afraid she'd only *dreamed* the library and the treasures it contained. But no. It was real. It was here. *She* was here.

"Oh, my. Oh, my goodness," the teapot said, her voice faltering.

"I *know*, Mrs. Potts. Isn't it *amazing*?" Belle exclaimed.

"Mon Dieu," said the feather duster, her tone dire. "I've never seen such a—a . . ."

"—wonderful, incredible, *astonishing* place!" Belle finished. "I agree, Plumette!"

Books were Belle's favorite things in the world. She devoured them. Villeneuve, her village, had a library, technically. But really it was just a shelf in Pere Robert's church. She'd read every book on it. Twice. But this library had so many books, she could never read them all. Not if she lived to be a thousand.

As she continued to look around, her eyes fell on the library's grand marble fireplace. She imagined herself sitting by it with a pot of tea and books stacked up all around her.

"Where will I start?" she wondered aloud. "With the Greek epics? The classical tragedies?"

"Might I suggest the windows?" Lumiere said, hurrying by her with rags draped over his arm.

Belle smiled sheepishly. His words brought her back down to earth. The windows were tall and graceful, but they were gray with grime. The draperies that framed them were in tatters. Cobwebs hung from the sills. She rolled up her sleeves, picked up her mop and bucket, and started toward them. As she did, the fringed footstool raced past her, stirring up a cloud of dust.

The little teacup was riding on its back. "Faster, Froufrou, faster!" he shouted in his little-boy voice.

"Chip! That's enough! You're making things worse!" Mrs. Potts scolded. "How on earth does the master work in here?" she added, poking her spout into a corner. A thick layer of dust carpeted much of the library's floor. It coated the large gilt table near the doorway, the chairs, the mantel.

Cogsworth ran a finger over a baseboard, inspected it, and paled.

"*Dust?* No one said anything about dust! I have delicate innards," he fretted, patting his casing. "Screws, posts, gears— one little speck in the works, and everything grinds to a halt!"

Lumiere wrinkled his nose. "That is *so* much more than we needed to know."

"I'll supervise, shall I?" offered Cogsworth. "To me, 'dust' is a four-letter word."

"'Dust' is a four-letter word to *everyone*," said Lumiere.

"'Work' is also a four-letter word," said Plumette, under her breath. "Perhaps *that* is why monsieur strives to avoid it?"

Cogsworth pulled himself up to his full height—all twelve inches of it. "I *heard* that, mademoiselle!" he thundered.

Plumette shook her feathers and flounced off to clean a chair.

Lumiere put an arm around a fuming Cogsworth. "Look,

old friend, I know the library's in a terrible state, and I know the task ahead seems impossible. But all we need to do is begin. The rest will take care of itself. A journey of a thousand miles starts with a single step."

"Quite right!" Cogsworth declared, barreling for the door. "I say we journey back to the kitchen, find a nice, cozy seat by the fire, and rethink the whole business."

But Lumiere intercepted him. He hooked his arm through Cogsworth's and turned him around.

"Belle can't do this alone. She needs our help," he said. "The library makes her happy. And we want her to be happy."

Cogsworth sighed. "My springs will never be the same."

Belle, overhearing their exchange, felt a stab of guilt. The servants had volunteered to help her at breakfast, but they hadn't known what they were getting into. While the library hadn't fallen to the same level of disrepair as the rest of the castle, it was still in need of a deep cleaning—one that Cogsworth didn't seem to be up to. His gears often got stuck and he frequently threw out his pendulum.

Worried, Belle hurried over to the two servants and knelt down. "Lumiere, Cogsworth," she said anxiously, "I can manage on my own. You have other things to do."

Cogsworth, who was already launching into another

round of griping, had the good grace to look abashed. He quickly tried to make amends.

"Would it make you happy, my dear?" he asked. "Having the use of this place?"

Belle nodded. "Very," she said.

"As happy as you were in your village?" he asked hopefully.

"My village?" Belle echoed, flustered by the question. She sat down on the floor. "Well, I didn't. . . . I mean, I wasn't. . . ."

How could she tell them the truth? It was hard enough to admit it to herself.

"What's the matter, child?" Cogsworth asked.

Mrs. Potts heard him. "Is something wrong?" she asked, hurrying over. Plumette followed, her feathers rustling. Even Chip and Froufrou stopped what they were doing and drew close to Belle.

Belle thought about making up an innocent fib or laughingly brushing aside their concern, but when she saw the worry in their eyes, genuine and deep, she knew she could do neither.

"The truth is, I *wasn't* happy in my village," she explained. "Not really. I was happy in my home, of course, with my father, but that was the only place I felt I belonged—there and in the pages of the books I read."

"Why, Belle?" Mrs. Potts asked.

Belle took a deep breath. "It was a small place. And the people . . . well, many of them had small hopes and small dreams. It was hard to find a friend there. There were so few people who understood me. My father did, of course. And Pere Robert, the clergyman with all of the books. And Agathe, a beggar woman. Everyone else thought I was odd," she admitted, blushing a little.

"You *are* odd, Belle," Chip piped up. "But we don't mind!"

Everyone laughed, even Belle. Only Mrs. Potts didn't. Instead, she raised a painted eyebrow.

"But Mama, she *is!*" Chip insisted. "She wears boots with a dress. And reads Latin. And rides her horse like a bandit!"

"Chip . . ." Mrs. Potts cautioned.

"It's not a *bad* thing, Mama. We're not exactly *normal*, you know. I mean, I'm a talking teacup!"

A wisp of steam rose from Mrs. Potts's spout.

"It's all right, Mrs. Potts," Belle said. "I suppose to the people of Villeneuve, I *was* odd. Because I wanted to leave. I wanted to travel and see something of the world." She smiled ruefully. "And because I liked books more than I liked Gaston."

"Gaston?" Lumiere echoed, a puzzled expression on his golden face.

"The village show-off," Belle replied, shaking her head at the memory of the handsome, preening braggart who had practically demanded that she marry him, then nearly fallen over backward when she had said no.

"Reading became my sanctuary," Belle continued. "I found so much in those books. I found histories that inspired me. Poems that delighted me. Novels that challenged me . . ." Belle paused, suddenly self-conscious. She looked down at her hands, and in a wistful voice, said, "What I really found, though, was myself."

Cogsworth, so full of complaints only moments ago, stepped forward and took Belle's hand.

"And you will find yourself *again*, child, in *this* library, if *I* have any say about it!" he declared, thrusting his chest out.

Belle looked up at him, surprised by the fervor in his voice.

"You have awoken this old soldier's martial spirit! We shall take back the library from the spiders and the mice! Once more unto the breach, dear friends! Never let it be said that Colonel Cogsworth of the Fourth Hussars backed down from a fight!"

He swiped a rag from the half dozen or so draped over Lumiere's arm and marched off, head held high, to do battle with the filthy windows.

"Colonel, is it now?" Lumiere remarked. "Last week it was

captain, and the week before lieutenant. He'll promote himself to brigadier general before long." He turned to Plumette. "Shall we, *cherie?*"

Plumette gave him a flirtatious smile, and together they attacked the dark corners, with Lumiere shining his candlelight over them and Plumette sweeping them clean.

Mrs. Potts joined Cogsworth at the windows. As she blew steam on the panes, Cogsworth rubbed the dirt away, his small brass arms working furiously. Even Froufrou and Chip helped. At Chip's request, Cogsworth tied rags to the footstool's four feet, and the two raced off again, dusting the floorboards as they careened around the room.

As Belle watched them all, a lump rose in her throat. They were so good to her. So kind. They wanted to help her. To make her happy. To be her friends.

And then there was the Beast.

A storm of conflicting emotions swept through her as she thought of him. He was the reason she was a captive in this dark, remote castle. He was also the reason she was standing in this incredible library.

The Beast wasn't like the others. Mrs. Potts, Lumiere, Plumette . . . they were warm and funny. Cheerful. Boisterous. He was difficult. Gruff. Enigmatic. Reclusive. And yet, in his own strange way, he wanted to make her happy, too. He'd proven that last night.

When Belle *thought* of what he'd done . . .

It was unbelievable. Impossible. Even now, it made her heart race.

Anyone else would have allowed her a glimpse of his collection. Loaned her a precious book or two. But the Beast, Belle was learning, was not anyone else.

She dunked her mop in her bucket now, squeezed it out, and started to clean in earnest. Unlike the Beast, she couldn't read, work, or do much of anything in the midst of a mess.

Belle didn't care if she finished at midnight. She didn't care if her muscles ached, her back groaned, and her legs wobbled from running up and down the stairs with buckets of water. She thought only about the happiness that awaited her once she finished her task.

For last night, the Beast had given her an unexpected present—a gift more valuable to her than his castle and all his lands, one more precious than jewels or gold.

Last night, the Beast had given her his books.

CHAPTER THREE

IT HAD HAPPENED AT DUSK.

Belle remembered it so clearly.

"I have a surprise for you," the Beast had said, in his usual brusque tone.

Belle had just come in from feeding her horse, Philippe, and was standing by the kitchen's back door, shaking snow from her cloak. She'd taken one look at him—at the scowl on his face, at his clenched paws, at his awkward stance—and said, "No, thank you."

The Beast had blinked, taken aback by her refusal. His scowl had deepened. "I *said* I have a surprise for you!"

"And I heard you," Belle had replied, "but I've had enough

surprises to last me a lifetime. Including cold, dark cells, packs of wolves, and tantrums."

"Tantrums? *Tantrums?*" the Beast had sputtered. "I can't believe . . . How can you say . . . That *wasn't* a *tantrum!* And it wasn't *my* fault! I told you not to go to the West Wing. I told you—"

Belle had given him a sidelong look. "You're right. What was I thinking? You'd *never* throw a tantrum. Now, if you'll excuse me, I need to hang up my cloak."

Things had been strained between the Beast and Belle ever since she'd gone to the West Wing in search of answers. A single rose had made her a captive, and she wanted to know why. When she asked the servants, all she got were evasive replies. From the Beast, she got nothing at all.

Fine, she'd thought. *If no one will give me any answers, I'll find them myself.*

The West Wing was the Beast's private domain. He'd forbidden Belle to venture there, and such a stern command, issued by such an imposing creature, would have been enough to frighten most people into unquestioning obedience.

But Belle was not most people. She questioned everything and was obedient to only one thing—her heart.

It had been dark in the Beast's chambers, but Belle's eyes had soon adjusted. As she'd moved through the once-beautiful rooms, she'd seen that all the fine furniture they contained had been broken; the costly bed hangings, shredded; the gilt mirrors, smashed.

"The Beast did this," she'd whispered.

She'd witnessed his anger, and knew he was more than capable of upending a table or flinging a chair across a room. Her eyes told her that the terrible destruction was borne of this anger. Her heart, however, saw its deeper cause—despair—and it ached for him.

Belle had continued to walk through the Beast's rooms, righting furniture, nudging shards of glass into a pile with her foot, looking for her answers.

Here I am, living in a remote castle, in a forest where it's always winter, she'd thought. *I talk to clocks. Joke with candlesticks. Play fetch with a barking footstool. That's what I do now. This is my life. There has to be a reason things are the way they are here. If only I can find out what it is.*

Ruined paintings hung on one wall, among them a portrait of a family: a man with a cold, imperious bearing; a woman with a warm smile and intelligent blue eyes; and a small boy who looked just like the woman.

Another portrait showed a handsome young man—blue-eyed, just like the boy. At least, Belle *thought* it showed a man. The portrait had been slashed so badly, the subject's eyes were almost all that remained.

"Who are you?" Belle had whispered.

But the painted faces had kept their silence. With a defeated sigh, she'd turned to go, no wiser than she had been when she'd entered the Beast's chambers.

And then she'd seen it—a single red rose. It was floating upright on a table, sheltered by a delicate glass cloche. Its head was drooping and several of its petals had fallen to the table. Belle had walked over to it, bent down, and peered through the cloche. As she'd watched, another petal dropped. Mesmerized, she lifted the glass to get a better look at the flower.

That's when the Beast had discovered her.

"What are you doing here? What did you do to it?" the Beast roared.

"N-nothing," Belle had stammered.

"Do you realize what you could have done? You could have damned us all! Get out! Go!" he'd raged, covering the rose with his form, upsetting Belle so badly that she'd fled from the Beast, the West Wing, and the castle.

She'd run to the stables, thrown a saddle on Philippe, and galloped away at breakneck speed. Through the woods they'd sped—straight into a pack of wolves. The vicious animals would have killed her if not for the Beast. She'd tried to fight them off herself, but there were too many. Just when she was certain they'd tear her apart, the Beast had come charging out come charging out of the woods and driven them away, but not before they'd wounded him badly.

With the help of Philippe, Belle had gotten the Beast back to the castle, tended to his wounds, and helped him to bed. She'd still been upset, though, and as the Beast had slept, fitfully tossing and turning, she'd asked Mrs. Potts how she and the other servants could stand by the Beast when he behaved so badly.

"Because he has a good heart," Mrs. Potts had said.

Belle had given her a look of disbelief. "Are we talking about the same Beast?" she'd asked.

Mrs. Potts had chuckled sadly, and then she'd sat Belle down and told her the Beast's story. He had been a prince, the son of a wealthy and powerful man, she'd said. His mother, who was kind and gentle, died when he was still a boy.

"Are those the people in the paintings?" Belle asked. "In the West Wing?"

"Yes, they are," Mrs. Potts had said.

She went on to explain that the Beast's father had been a cruel man who'd abused his only child.

Belle had been shocked to learn that, and filled with sorrow. Her mother had died young, too, when Belle was only a baby, but unlike the Beast's father, her father had been kindness itself.

"How frightened he must've been, and lonely, and sad. A poor, motherless boy in the hands of such a brutal man," she'd said.

Mrs. Potts had nodded, her eyes downcast. "After years of such terrible treatment, the prince grew up to be as callous and thoughtless and selfish as his father had been," she'd said. "And then one day, he threw an extravagant ball and invited the most beautiful ladies of the realm to attend. In the midst of the dancing, a beggar woman entered the ballroom and asked the prince for shelter from the wind and rain. He laughed at her and told his guards to throw her out. But the old woman was really an enchantress. She cursed the prince, turning him into a beast. She cursed us, his servants, too. And from that day on, we've been like this. Unable to go back to our old selves, and our old lives."

"I'm so sorry, Mrs. Potts," Belle said, heartsick for her friend.

"So am I, child. So am I."

"Is there nothing you can do?"

Mrs. Potts turned her gaze to the Beast. When she spoke again, her voice was faraway. "You have so many questions, child. And who wouldn't? Let me at least answer your first one: we stay with our master because we will not abandon him twice."

"Twice?" Belle had repeated. "I don't understand."

"We knew how terrible his father was to him, and yet we did nothing," Mrs. Potts had said, clearly distressed by the admission. "That man was the true beast, and we were too frightened to stand up to him. Our master needs us now as much as he did then, and this time we will not forsake him."

Belle had pressed. "I want to help you. There must be some way to lift the curse."

The Beast had groaned in his sleep then, and Mrs. Potts had rushed to his side.

"It's not for you to worry about, lamb," Mrs. Potts had said. "We've made our bed and we must lie in it."

The Beast and Belle had traded some sharp words that night, both before the wolf attack and after, and they hadn't talked much since, which was why Belle had been in no mood for his surprise.

After she'd turned him down, she'd walked through the kitchen intending to find Chapeau, the coatrack, and hand him her cloak. As she did, Cogsworth and Mrs. Potts exchanged concerned glances. Cuisinier, the cookstove, was so worried, he started to smoke.

Lumiere had hurried over to the Beast. Cupping a hand to his mouth, he'd leaned in close and said, "Might I suggest, master, that you employ a smile and a friendly tone of voice to indicate that this is a *happy* surprise, and not, say, a trip to the guillotine?"

His words had been spoken in low tones, but Belle had heard them nonetheless. Sound carried in the vast kitchen, with its high vaulted ceilings.

The Beast had cleared his throat. "Belle!" he'd called after her. "I have a very nice, splendid, rather wonderful surprise for you!"

He'd sounded so bright and enthusiastic, so unlike his usual self, that Belle had stopped short and turned around just to make sure that it was really the Beast who'd spoken.

It was. He'd been standing right where she'd left him, smiling at her—or trying to. The expression had more closely resembled a grimace and had made him look even fiercer than he usually did, despite the fact that he'd taken care with his appearance and was beautifully dressed.

He'd been wearing a linen shirt, a ruffled cravat, and a coat made of silk. A pair of fierce black horns swept back from his temples. Fur covered his face and body, and hair like a lion's mane cascaded down his back. His paws were massive; his claws long and sharp. He was tall and powerfully built.

But the most arresting thing about the Beast was not his size or his strength: it was his eyes. They were not golden like a tiger's, or deep brown like a bear's. They were a clear, piercing blue—as deep as a mountain lake, and every bit as unfathomable. Like all wild creatures, the Beast guarded his gaze, wary of making eye contact, of revealing too much.

"It *is* nice, Belle. I promise," he'd said. "Won't you at least come see it?"

Something about his expression, hopeful and helpless at the same time, had softened Belle.

He's trying, she'd thought. *They all are. Should I?*

"No yelling, or roaring, or growling . . ." she'd warned.

The Beast had nodded solemnly. He'd held out his paw.

Belle had stared at it, deliberating. Then, with a nod of her head, she'd taken it.

CHAPTER FOUR

"YOUR EYES ARE CLOSED?"

"You've asked me five times."

"You can't see anything?"

"Not with a blindfold on."

Belle had been standing in front of a pair of tall, gracefully arched doors. The Beast had led her out of the kitchen, down a long corridor, and up a flight of stone steps. When they'd arrived, he'd put the candelabrum he'd been carrying down on a table next to the doors. Then he'd insisted on tying his cravat around her eyes.

"Wait there," he'd said when he was finished. "Don't wander off."

Belle had laughed. *"Wander off?* Near a staircase? In a blindfold?"

The Beast hadn't responded. He'd been too busy fumbling with a brass key ring. Belle had heard the keys jangling.

Why is it taking him so long to fit a key into a lock? she'd wondered. *Surely he knows how to open the doors of his own castle.*

And then she'd realized why: he was nervous.

He wants me to like the surprise, she'd thought. *He wants to please me.*

The thought of the Beast wanting to please *anyone* was so odd, Belle had immediately dismissed it. There must be another reason. Maybe the light was bad wherever they were. Maybe he couldn't see the keys.

"Ah! Here we go!" the Beast had finally said.

Belle had heard the key turn and the hinges groan. She'd felt a rush of musty air against her face as the doors swung open. She'd smelled leather. And linseed oil, a component of paints and inks.

"This way," the Beast had said, leading her forward. "Careful, Belle . . . just a little farther . . . stop right here!"

Belle had tilted her head toward him, intrigued by his voice. There were things in it she hadn't heard before: anticipation, excitement, happiness.

"Where *are* we?" she'd asked, eager to know what sort of place would bring out such emotions in him.

"Be patient. You'll see," he'd said. "We just need a bit of light first."

Belle had heard him walk back through the doorway and grab the candelabrum.

"Are you ready?" he'd asked, by her side again.

"I *think* so," Belle had replied.

The Beast had untied the blindfold. "All right, Belle," he'd said. "Open your eyes."

Belle had, blinking.

Her eyes had grown round. Her hands had come up to her mouth.

In the light of the candelabrum, she'd seen them—*books.* Hundreds of them. *Thousands.*

The Beast had brought her to his library. It was dark and dusty, in need of a good cleaning, but it was still one of the most awe-inspiring rooms she'd ever seen. The ceiling was two stories high. Tall shelves lined the walls. Wooden ladders mounted on brass rails allowed visitors access to the highest reaches. A carved marble mantel, nestled between the shelves along one wall, was flanked by two deep leather chairs.

"Do you like the surprise, Belle?" the Beast had asked.

"Like it?" Belle had said, a catch in her voice. "I *love* it."

Captivated by the books, Belle didn't see the Beast smile. She didn't see his eyes, so hidden, so haunted, fill with a pale, fragile hope.

Belle pulled a book down from the nearest shelf and blew dust off its cover.

The book's binding, of fine calfskin, was as soft as a glove. Belle had opened it and had seen that its endpapers were colorfully marbled and its pages beautifully printed with a rich black ink. No wonder she'd recognized the scents of leather and linseed when she entered the room. Together, they made the beguiling perfume of a book.

The Beast had joined her. He'd squinted at the title. *"The Faerie Queene,"* he'd said. "A poem written for England's Queen Elizabeth, and one of my favorites."

"Mine, too!" said Belle.

The Beast had cleared his throat. " 'For whatsoever from one place doth fall, is with the tide unto an other brought. . . .' "

Delighted, Belle had spoken the next line. " 'For there is nothing lost . . .' "

" 'That may be found, if sought,' " they'd finished, together.

Belle's brown eyes had shone with happiness. All her life, she'd loved books. She loved the look of them, the smell of them, the sweet weight of them in her arms. Most of all, she loved the feeling she got every time she picked one up—the feeling of holding an entire world in her hands.

She'd put *The Faerie Queene* back, crossed the room to a different shelf, and pulled another book from it. *"Renaissance Splendors of Venice,"* she'd said, reading its title aloud. "Your library is extraordinary. It's amazing. Thank you so much for bringing me here."

"I'm glad you like it. It's my favorite place in the entire castle. I come here every day. My great-great-grandfather started it," the Beast had explained. "His most prized acquisition was an original quarto of *Hamlet.*"

"Shakespeare!" Belle had exclaimed. "He's my favorite! Do you have more of his work?" she'd asked. *"The Tempest? Romeo and Juliet?"*

"Yes, of course. All of Shakespeare's work is here. There's also an excellent selection of poetry, and you may come across the odd enchanted book, too. Most are harmless, but one or two can be a little unruly." He'd paused. "But this is silly. Instead of me telling you what's here, go see for yourself."

That was all Belle had needed to hear. In a heartbeat, she was off, bounding from bookcase to bookcase, her boots leaving prints in the dust.

What stories this place contains! she'd thought. *Stories of triumph and defeat, love and betrayal. Stories of sorrow and joy.*

There were lives between all the covers—bold, brilliant ones. There were exotic, faraway places. All she had to do was open a book to become Joan of Arc at the Siege of Orléans, Marco Polo traveling the Silk Road, or Cleopatra sailing to Tarsus to meet Mark Antony. She might be a captive, but in this room, with a book in her hand, she could be free.

"Come here anytime, Belle. Read whatever you like. These books are yours now," the Beast had said softly. "They're my gift to you."

Belle had laughed. The Beast was joking; he had to be. This collection was incomparable. It was priceless. No one would simply give it away.

"If I could borrow one or two?" she'd asked, looking up at a shelf.

But she'd received no answer.

Puzzled by the silence, Belle had turned around, and had seen that she was talking to herself.

The Beast had gone.

CHAPTER FIVE

BELLE HAD STOOD THERE for a long moment, staring at the empty doorway.

The gift the Beast had bestowed upon her was so incredibly generous, it was almost unbelievable. She felt as if the Beast, who had caused her so much sorrow, was now doing everything in his power to undo it.

Everything, that is, except letting her go.

"Who are you?" she'd whispered.

Was the Beast the snarling savage who'd imprisoned her father, then herself? Was he the cultivated reader who could recite lines from a sixteenth-century poem? Was he her adversary? Her friend?

Or was he somehow all of these things?

As ever, Belle had only questions. Mrs. Potts had answered many of them the night Belle had fled the castle, but she'd left others unanswered, including the most important one: Why was she, Belle, here?

Belle was certain that the answer to that question was also the key to her liberty. But until she could obtain it, books would be her escape.

A volley of loud barks tore Belle from her thoughts of the recent past and brought her back to the present.

Froufrou and Chip were still racing back and forth, only now Chip was now wearing a dust rag tied around his rim like a pirate's scarf and threatening Froufrou with a keelhauling. They crashed into Belle's mop bucket, causing it to slosh water all over the floor.

Mrs. Potts scolded her son. "Chip, wipe that water up, please. Then find a book and a corner to read it in. Right now. Or you're going to the kitchen to help Cuisinier prepare tonight's dinner!"

"Pah! I'm not a measuring cup, Mama, I'm Captain Kidd, scourge of the high seas!" Chip retorted.

"Scourge of high *tea*, perhaps," said a voice from the doorway.

It was the Beast. The servants all stopped what they were

doing to bow or curtsy. Even Chip and Froufrou made an attempt to shape up.

"No, no . . . please. Carry on," the Beast said. "You're doing a fine job. The library is looking so much better."

Belle noticed that he looked a little awkward, even a little shy. As if he were an intruder in this lively, busy place.

As she and the others resumed their tasks, the Beast patted Froufrou, then bent down to Chip and said, "I, um . . . I don't know if you'd be interested, but there's a wonderful book on pirates in the back of the library. Right side. On the shelf below the window seat."

Chip's eyes lit up. "Thank you!" he said, zooming off to find it—and forgetting to wipe up the spilled water.

The Beast straightened, then walked through the library, paws behind his back, nodding approvingly at the work being done.

"Lumiere," he said, pointing at a corner. "You missed a spot."

"Why, thank you, master," Lumiere said, hurrying to wipe away a bit of dust he'd overlooked.

The Beast nodded, clearly pleased at being helpful. "Cogsworth!" he said, a few seconds later, tapping a mahogany table.

"Master?"

"There's a streak of wax on this."

"Very good, master," Cogsworth said between gritted teeth, as he hurried to the table with a rag.

The Beast bounced on his heels, smiling. "Mrs. Potts!" he called out. "There's still a spot of tarnish on that doorknob!"

"How very kind of master to point it out," Mrs. Potts said, steam rising from her spout.

Belle, mopping by a bookshelf, stole a glance at the Beast. As she watched, he pushed up his sleeves, then grabbed a rag and bucket.

Uh-oh, she thought.

Lumiere, Cogsworth, Plumette, and Mrs. Potts all watched with trepidation as the Beast started toward a window. He dunked his rag into the water and proceeded to rub the dripping cloth over the grimy panes.

"There! What do you think, Lumiere?" he asked a few minutes later.

Belle bit her lip to keep from laughing. The window was twice as dirty as it had been when he started.

"What do I think?" Lumiere said, struggling for words. "I think, master, that . . . that your . . ."

Cogsworth raised a hand to his mouth. *"Enthusiasm,"* he coughed.

"I think your *enthusiasm* is an example to us all!" Lumiere exclaimed, his candle flames flaring brightly.

"Excellent!" the Beast said, beaming. "I'll clean another one!"

Before Lumiere could discourage him, Chip—obviously having found the pirate book—came tearing around the corner after Froufrou. "Arrr! Ye scurvy dog!" he shouted. "Time to walk the plank!"

A small smile crossed the Beast's face. He picked up a mop, pretended it was a sword, and brandished it at Chip. "En garde, pirate knave!"

Chip jumped onto Froufrou's back. "You'll never take me alive!" he shouted.

The Beast advanced, thrusting the mop handle at his adversaries. Froufrou growled. He crouched down, then charged.

Feigning alarm, the Beast beat a hasty retreat. He backed up across the library's floor, fending off the pirate marauders with his mop . . . and never saw the cake of soap on the floor, lying in a puddle of spilled water.

CHAPTER SIX

IT HAPPENED SO FAST, Belle didn't even have time to blink.

The Beast's foot came down on the cake of soap. He skidded backward, arms windmilling. His other foot hit a bucket full of dirty water and launched it into the air. He fell against a bookcase. Wood splintered. The shelves broke. Books rained down. The mop snapped. And the bucket landed, upside down, on his head.

There were a few seconds of shocked silence. Then Belle threw her own mop down.

"Are you all right?" she cried.

The Beast sat up, looking this way and that, the bucket

still on his head. Belle ran to him, knelt down, and pulled it off. He blinked up at her, bedraggled, shamefaced, and furious. Filthy water dripped from his fur. Without thinking, he shook himself vigorously

Belle, still on her knees, was so close to him, that she got doused. "Oh!" she cried. "Yuck!"

The others got wet, too. Cogsworth sputtered. Plumette shook her dripping feathers. Mrs. Potts and Chip made faces as beads of gray water rolled down their porcelain surfaces.

And the Beast growled. It was a low, frightening sound, a harbinger of yet another angry outburst. The smiling, playful master of a few moments ago was gone. In his place was an angry, embarrassed creature, desperate to recover his dignity.

The servants sensed the coming storm. Lumiere hurried to avert it. He cleared his throat. Water was dripping down his face. Wisps of smoke were rising from his extinguished candles. He steepled his hands together, mustered a bright smile, and said, "You are an incredible help, master. Invaluable. But I wonder if perhaps your time might be better spent studying the Roman stoics? Reacquainting yourself with the Persian poets? Brushing up on the ancient Greek philosophers?"

The Beast's growl deepened. He opened his mouth, ready to snap at Lumiere and the others, but before he could, another sound was heard—musical and tinkling, except for the odd honk or snort.

It was Belle. She was sitting back on her heels, her hands on her knees, laughing her head off.

The Beast turned to her. "Stop it! Stop laughing at me!" he snapped.

Belle recoiled, taken aback by his tone. "I'm *not* laughing at you," she retorted.

"No?" said the Beast acidly. "Well, you certainly aren't laughing *with* me."

Belle shook her head. "You're right, I'm not. I'd like to laugh with you, but it's impossible unless *you* laugh," she said, a hint of irritation in her own voice now.

"This is *not* funny, Belle."

"Yes, it is. No one was hurt. We're all fine. Look at *me*. My hair's stuck to my head. I'm covered in dirty water. My clothes are wet. Everyone else looks awful, too," she said gesturing at the servants. "And if you could've seen yourself, skidding across the floor—"

She started to giggle again, but a snarl from the Beast cut her off. Belle was very close to him, only inches away. So close that he couldn't hide his eyes from her, as he usually did. She looked into them, expecting to see anger. Instead, she saw a painful vulnerability.

He thinks I'm being unkind, Belle thought. *That I'm making fun of him.*

An image flashed into her mind of his chambers, and the destruction he'd wreaked within them. She remembered the sense of despair she'd felt in those rooms. And the story Mrs. Potts had told her about the Beast's childhood. His wounds were still deep, still raw.

Why do you care? a voice inside her asked. *Did the Beast care when he made your father a prisoner in this castle? And then made you one?*

Belle did not answer the voice, not right away. Instead, she thought of her father.

Once when she was little, they had gone walking in the woods. They'd come across a vixen, her leg caught in a cruel steel trap. Belle's father had set about trying to free her, but the poor fox, mad with pain and fear, had lunged at him. Over and over again, he'd tried to help the suffering animal. And over and over again, she'd attacked him.

"Papa, stop!" Belle had finally cried, scared for him. "She's going to bite you!"

"Hush, Belle," he'd said. "The fox cannot change her nature and I cannot change mine."

Slowly, patiently, he'd persisted, until finally, the exhausted vixen had sunk down on the ground. He'd been able to open the trap then, and free her.

Why do you care? the voice asked again.

Belle answered it by reaching into her pocket. She'd stuffed a rag into it earlier, as she was gathering cleaning supplies. It was still dry; the wetness from her clothing had not yet seeped through to it.

She pulled it out now and started to rub at the Beast's wet face. Her touch was gentle, yet he flinched at it as if she'd struck him.

"What are you doing?" he asked, his voice uncertain now instead of angry.

"What does it look like I'm doing? I'm wiping your face."

"You don't need to. It's not necessary. I'm quite all right," he protested. "That's too rough. Ow. Stop. You're pulling my fur out. Be careful! That's my nose, you know. Ow. *Ow!* My ears are very tender!"

Belle persisted, ignoring his complaints. "Better?" she asked, when she was done.

"I suppose so. Yes. Somewhat," the Beast replied grudgingly. "But my coat's filthy and my shirt's soaked. I-I shall go to my bedroom to change. And then to my study. I've been working on a translation of Epictetus. I must make some progress on it, you know. I can't be expected to dillydally here all day."

He stood up, shook water from his paws, and walked to

the doorway. He paused there for a few awkward seconds and cast a last, longing glance around the library.

He wishes he could stay here, Belle thought. *With us. He'd rather mop a dirty floor than be alone in his chambers.*

"Chapeau? *Chapeau!* Fetch me some clean clothes!" he bellowed.

Belle heard the coatrack come clattering down the hall. He appeared in the doorway and did a double take at the sight of the Beast. He pressed two of his hands to his skinny chest and threw the rest of them up in the air, distraught at the sight of his master's attire.

"Now, now, Chapeau. You mustn't overreact," the Beast said. "All messes, accidents, and catastrophes are to be blithely laughed off." He looked pointedly at Belle. "Or so I'm told."

Chapeau rushed the Beast out of the library and off to his chambers, and Belle and the servants were left to themselves.

Still kneeling, Belle stuffed the damp rag into her pocket, then started to pick up the books that had fallen to the floor when the Beast crashed into the bookcase.

"We'll have to find some empty shelves where we can put these volumes," she said to the servants. "Has anyone seen any?"

No one replied.

That's odd, Belle thought, turning to look at them.

They were right there, standing stock-still. Not one of

them had budged since the Beast had left the room. They gazed at the empty doorway as if in a daze.

"Plumette? Mrs. Potts? Is something wrong?" Belle asked, puzzled by their strange behavior.

"The master was angry . . ." Lumiere started.

"But he didn't shout," Plumette finished, amazement in her voice.

"He didn't roar," added Cogsworth.

"Or break a single *thing*," said Mrs. Potts, wonderingly. "It must be because . . ."

She glanced at Lumiere, then Cogsworth, looking as if she'd said too much. Her words trailed away.

"Because of what?" Belle eagerly asked, hoping she might learn something, anything, that would help her understand why she was here.

But Mrs. Potts disappointed her. She merely said, "Because he has to get back to his work."

Frustration gripped Belle. She wanted to press her for more information, but she knew it would get her nowhere. Mrs. Potts was already back at the windows, steaming them clean. This always happened. The servants always found something to do or somewhere to be when she asked the wrong questions.

Belle felt a crushing loneliness descend on her. The Beast

was gone, and the servants had all returned to their tasks. She suddenly missed her father terribly. Thinking about the time they'd discovered the fox in the trap had made her yearn for his company. If only she could talk to him. Even if it was just for an hour. But she knew that was not going to happen. Not now. Not ever.

Refusing to give in to her feelings of hopelessness, Belle picked up half a dozen books off the floor and looked for a place to put them.

She reminded herself that she was much better off than she had been a day ago. She had the Beast's library now. She might be lonely—being a captive in a strange castle where it was always winter could make anyone feel lonely. But she wasn't alone. She had Shakespeare for company now. Molière. Dante. Rousseau.

She would find out the truth behind her captivity. Maybe not today or tomorrow, but one day she would.

And until then, she would take comfort in books.

Just as she always had.

CHAPTER SEVEN

"I'VE PUT A CRICK IN MY SPRINGS," said Cogsworth direly, his hands pressed to the back of his casing. "I fear I shall never chime properly again."

It was four o'clock. Dusk was settling over the castle. Belle and her friends had been cleaning for eight hours, with only a short break.

"An easy chair and a rest by the fire will put you to rights, Mr. Cogsworth," said Mrs. Potts. "I set out some oil to ease your gears, and fluffed a nice, soft pillow for you."

"Dear woman, you are an angel of mercy!" Cogsworth exclaimed. He bent down to pick up a rag off the floor, wincing as he did, then headed for the door.

"Cogsworth, wait!" Belle said, running to catch up with him.

He stopped and turned around. "Do *not* tell me I missed a spot!" he cautioned.

"May I tell you thank you?" she asked, kneeling down to kiss his cheek.

Cogsworth smiled. "That you may, my darling girl," he said, patting her arm.

"And you, too, Mrs. Potts, Plumette, Lumiere," Belle added, looking at each of her friends in turn. "It would have taken me a month to do all this work by myself. You were all so kind to help, and it means so much to me."

"It was our pleasure," Lumiere said.

"Hardly!" grumbled Plumette. She looked around, assessing their work. "But the place *does* look very nice."

Cogsworth, rag in hand, walked stiffly out of the library. Belle could hear his groans carrying up from the stairwell. Plumette and Lumiere trailed after him.

Mrs. Potts followed, then turned back in the doorway. Her eyes traveled from Belle's face to her boots and back again. "If you could see yourself, child!" she said, chuckling. "You look as if you've been crawling up chimneys all day!"

Belle laughed. She stuffed the dust rag she was still holding into her skirt pocket.

"Are you not coming down? I've put the kettle on for tea," Mrs. Potts said.

"Perhaps in a moment," Belle said, gazing past Mrs. Potts at a shelf full of books.

Mrs. Potts smiled. "I quite understand. Tea and biscuits aren't as tempting as stories, not for a bookworm. Do come down for some dinner, though, child. The master's eating in his study tonight, so dinner will only be a simple affair, but we'll fix you something nourishing. You need a good meal after all the work you've done."

Belle promised she would, and Mrs. Potts went downstairs to join the others. As soon as she was gone, Belle turned and looked at the library. *Her* library. The floorboards had been polished to a deep shine. A fire was burning in the hearth. Every single inch of shelving had been dusted. The cobwebs were gone. The windows were gleaming.

She picked up a candlestick and walked along a wall of towering bookcases, running her fingers over spines, eyeing titles, feeling as if she were the richest person in the world.

When she came to the end of the row, she saw the window seat. A book lay open on its thick velvet cushion—a book on pirates.

"*Chip*," Belle said, shaking her head.

She put her candle down, picked the book up, and put it

away. As she did, her eyes fell upon a narrow wooden door tucked between two tall bookcases catty-corner from the window seat.

It was slightly ajar.

Belle hadn't cleaned whatever was on the other side. She'd been so busy at the front of the library, she hadn't even seen the door. Had anyone else?

"Crumbs," she sighed. "Don't tell me we missed an entire room."

Holding her candle out in front of her, Belle walked to the door. She grasped the knob, and as she did—a sense of dread, heavy and chilling as winter fog, descended on her. She felt her body go cold and quickly drew her hand away.

"Stop it, you goose," she said aloud, annoyed by her silly behavior. "Get hold of yourself."

Pushing the door open, she stepped into a small, dark room. It was even dustier than the rest of the library had been. Shining her candle around it, she saw that there was nothing sinister in the room at all—only a desk upon which lay quills, an empty inkpot, a dried-up pot of glue, paper, cloth, and a thick ledger with the word ACQUISITIONS written on it.

The room had obviously been used to catalog new books and repair old ones. Perhaps the castle had had its own librarian once. Belle smiled to think that *she* was a librarian now.

She vowed to keep a well-organized, tidy library—one that would make Pere Robert proud.

She opened the ancient ledger. Its last entry, written in a neat, precise hand, described a first edition of Dante's *The Divine Comedy*, purchased from a bookseller in Venice for a princely sum.

Belle's heart quickened at the thought of holding such a precious, priceless book in her hand, but Dante would have to wait until tomorrow. She was too tired to even open a book right now, much less hunt for one.

She closed the ledger, and as she did, a ghostly wail rose behind her. She spun around, gasping with fright, but soon saw the cause. The room's only window was slightly open, and the winter wind was whistling through. A coating of snow had blown onto the sill.

Belle shivered. She put her candle down and closed the window. The idea of sitting by a cheerful fire in the kitchen with a cup of tea and her friends for company suddenly seemed quite appealing. She picked up her candle and was just about to leave the workroom when something else caught her eye—a heavy black book resting on a table to the left of the window.

"That's strange. Why aren't you shelved?" she wondered aloud, walking over to it.

The book's leather binding was oddly free of dust. Had someone come in here to read it? Had the Beast left it out for her?

She looked at the floor, but the only footprints in the dust were her own. Frowning, she bent down to the book. Its title was stamped on the cover in gold.

"*'Nevermore,'*" she read aloud. Intrigued, she picked it up.

The book was warm. Belle felt a faint pulsing as she touched it. As if it had a heartbeat. As if it were alive. Startled, she dropped it.

It landed on the table with a loud thump.

Then it snapped upright.

CHAPTER EIGHT

BELLE TOOK A STEP BACK. She was used to objects that talked and moved now, but she hadn't expected the book to be one of them.

The Beast had warned her that the library contained a few enchanted books, and that some of them tended to be unruly. Was this one? What was it going to do?

"I-I'm sorry I disturbed you," Belle said hesitantly. "I didn't mean to."

The book didn't respond to her apology. Instead, it moved to the edge of the table, walking on its bottom corners, and jumped down.

Belle moved farther away, but as she did, her heel caught

in the rug. She lost her balance and fell on the floor with a hard, jarring thud.

For a few seconds, she thought it was her new perspective that made *Nevermore* look bigger than it had.

But as her head cleared, she saw that she was wrong.

The book was growing.

CHAPTER NINE

AS BELLE WATCHED, saucer-eyed, *Nevermore* expanded.

Taller and taller it grew, until it towered over her. When it was nearly touching the ceiling, it stopped growing, and then its front cover swung open, ever so slightly, and sounds spilled out of it: a woman's laughter, a man's shout, horses whinnying, music, glasses clinking.

Belle didn't know whether to feel scared or thrilled. And then she saw something—something spidery and black crouching in the shadow between *Nevermore's* cover and its pages. It darted out of the book and crawled up a wall. Another scurried up the side of the desk. A third jumped onto a bookshelf.

Belle, still sitting on the floor, scuttled backward, away from the creatures. *What are they?* she wondered warily. *Bugs? Mice?*

The cover opened wider and more of the creatures crawled out. Belle scrambled to her feet, ready to stamp them away if they came close.

But then one did, and Belle's wariness turned to wonder as she saw what it was. Not an insect or a rodent, but a *word*.

She knelt down and put her hand on the floor, palm up. EAGER jumped onto it. OAF ran over her toes. CERTAIN chased DUBIOUS around the room. PRECIOUS and EXQUISITE shoved each other.

The room was filling up with words. They spilled out of the book like water tumbling down a streambed. They curled around her ankles and tugged on the hem of her skirt.

Belle put EAGER down. As she did, *Nevermore*'s cover creaked all the way open. Its pages started turning, slowly at first, then faster, blowing Belle's hair back, plastering her skirts to her legs. Then they abruptly stopped. And the book remained open to a page with only five words on it: THE COUNTESS GIVES A PARTY.

That page slowly turned, and Belle caught her breath, astonished by what she saw.

There were no words on the paper, just a picture that

took up the entire page. As Belle looked at it, the picture came to life. Dancers whirled. An orchestra played. Belle smelled perfume, wine, and roses.

People, she thought. A longing as deep as hunger filled her as she realized how much she missed human faces, laughter, and conversation.

She walked up to the page and touched it. It rippled and sparkled under her fingers like the surface of a sun-dappled pond. Mesmerized, she pushed her arm into it all the way up to her elbow, then pulled it back out. Droplets of silvery light clung to her skin like melted candlewax, then hardened in the air. When she shook them off, they landed on the wooden floor, sparkling like diamonds.

"What are you?" she murmured to the book.

As if answering her, the page rippled again. The book seemed to be beckoning to her. She'd put her arm into the silver with no ill effect. . . . What if she stepped into the book? Was that even possible?

Belle's heartbeat quickened with excitement at the thought of walking into *Nevermore's* pages and finding out where the laughter and music were coming from, but something held her back. What was inside those pages? What if she didn't like it there? How would she get back?

She remembered what the Beast had told her about the enchanted books. *Most are harmless, but one or two can be a little unruly.*

If I can handle the Beast, I can handle unruly, she thought.

Then she took a deep breath.

And stepped into the story.

CHAPTER TEN

"MADEMOISELLE! LOOK OUT!" A voice cried.

Belle turned around. Her heart lurched. She screamed.

A carriage drawn by four enormous gray horses was bearing down on her out of the darkness. She leapt out of the way, flattening herself against a prickly hedge. The carriage flew past her and disappeared.

Shaking with fright, Belle pressed a hand to her chest. Had the driver called out a split second later, she would've been trampled.

"Where am I?" she whispered, looking all around.

Nevermore stood upright, only a few paces away, its pages shimmering. But the library's workroom was gone.

"The book must be some sort of portal," Belle reasoned. "A doorway from the library to here. Wherever *here is*."

It was nighttime, and as Belle's eyes adjusted, she saw that she was standing in a graveled drive. Candles flickered in lanterns lining its edges. The drive appeared to cut through a vast estate, its grounds dotted by huge, leafy oaks, yew trees, rosebushes, and shrubs cut in the shape of animals.

Still trembling, Belle looked to her left and saw a pair of tall iron gates, open to let carriages through. A coat of arms was emblazoned on them. It showed two crossed scythes with a motto printed underneath them: OMNIA VINCO.

Belle had learned a bit of Latin at her village's tiny library. "'I conquer all,'" she read aloud. *The property must belong to a general, admiral, or powerful nobleman,* she thought.

The gates were anchored to high stone pillars. Thick walls sloped off from them, and statues stood atop them: one of Hades, god of the underworld, the other of Persephone, his wife. Outside the gates lay a vast, inky darkness.

Belle looked to her right, down the long drive, and saw a golden light shining through the trees.

Just then another carriage approached, this one drawn by four high-stepping white horses. Belle, standing safely out of the way now, watched as it, too, sped down the drive.

She cast an uncertain glance at the enchanted book,

trying to decide what to do. Part of her wanted to step right back through its pages to the security of the Beast's castle, but another, more adventurous part wanted to find out where those carriages were going and what was giving off that golden light.

The adventurous part won out, as it usually did, and Belle set off down the drive at a brisk pace. It curved and dipped as it wound through the estate, leading Belle past heavily wooded patches, ponds and streams, thickets and brambles. There were times when she lost sight of the light altogether and wondered what she'd gotten herself into, but she stayed on the drive and doggedly kept walking. A good quarter hour after she started out, she emerged from a copse of slender birch trees and stopped dead, amazed.

Before her stood an immense château, a breathtaking Baroque confection, ablaze with candlelight.

Painted carriages had pulled up to its sweeping staircase— the drivers straight-backed, the horses tossing their heads. The people alighting from them were the most dazzling crea- tures Belle had ever seen. Their faces were powdered; their lips rouged. Some wore tiny fabric beauty marks on their cheeks. Women wore gowns in all the colors of a summer gar- den, and men sported silk frock coats and matching breeches. Gemstone buttons winked from their waistcoats.

CHAPTER TEN

Footmen in livery announced the arrival of royalty and foreign dignitaries. Belle watched, wide-eyed, as a Japanese princess, the shah of Persia, a Russian count, and an ambassador from England ascended the stairs.

They all looked so exotic and fascinating, and Belle yearned to speak with them, to hear about their lives and learn about their countries. Until she'd journeyed to the Beast's castle, Belle had never been out of Villeneuve. Kyoto, Shiraz, St. Petersburg, London—how incredibly exotic those faraway cities were compared with her dull, tiny village.

With a quick glance around to make sure no one was watching her, Belle scurried closer. She had no right to enter these premises, but she couldn't help herself. She wanted to drink in every glittering detail. As she hugged the edge of the drive, trying to stay in the shadows, she heard people call out greetings to one another and saw men bow to women and kiss their hands.

Captivated, she moved closer still. A row of cherry trees fanned out from either side of the mansion's steps. Belle darted to the one closest to the house, hiding under the lacy branches. She wrapped her arms around the tree's slender trunk and pressed her cheek against it, aching to join all the beautiful people. But she knew it was a ridiculous wish.

"What a contrast I'd make to the elegant company," she

said ruefully, looking down at her clothing. "In my filthy dress, with my dusty . . ."

Boots, she was about to say, but the word died in her throat.

Her blue work dress was gone. In its place was a shimmering silk ball gown.

CHAPTER ELEVEN

BELLE RELEASED THE CHERRY TREE. She looked around wildly.

"How . . . how did this happen?" she stammered.

Stunned, she touched her dress to make sure it was real. The silk rustled under her hands. She looked at her feet. Her leather boots had been replaced by delicate satin slippers. Her hands went to her hair. It was styled high up on her head. They fluttered to her neck. A cluster of jewels rested against her collarbones.

"Sapphires," she said, looking down at them. "I'm wearing *sapphires.*"

No one in Villeneuve owned *one* sapphire, never mind the flawless dozens set in the exquisite necklace.

The sudden transformation was dizzying. Belle squeezed her eyes shut and counted to ten, certain that when she opened them, she would be wearing her old blue dress again. But no.

Still unable to believe what had happened, Belle stepped out from under the tree into the light emanating from the château, the better to see herself. She didn't realize it, but she was now standing so close to the staircase that she could have reached out and touched one of the stone lions lying at its base.

A group of guests, high-spirited and laughing, walked past her. One of them, a young woman, looked her up and down. "What a gorgeous gown!" she said, hooking her arm through Belle's. "Do tell me the name of your dressmaker!" she begged, pulling Belle up the stairs and into the foyer.

"My gown? Th-this one?" Belle stuttered, wondering how she would answer her.

Luckily, she didn't have to. A young man came up to them and whispered something in the woman's ear. She burst into laughter and swatted him with her fan, releasing Belle, then seemed to forget all about her as the young man led her away.

CHAPTER ELEVEN

The opulent entryway was thronged with people. Music rose over their laughter. Candles flickered crazily. The scent of roses was heady. Arched doorways led off the foyer in three different directions; another sweeping staircase led to the upper levels. Belle started to panic. She didn't know which way to go or what to do.

"Mademoiselle, may I?" said a voice.

Belle turned to her right and looked into a pair of amused gray eyes. They belonged to a young man, perhaps only a year or two older than she was. He was wearing a pale green frock coat. His thick dark hair was pulled back and tied with a black ribbon, and a half-smile played about his lips.

"It would be my sincere pleasure to escort you," he said.

"Escort me where?" Belle asked, dazed.

"Why, to meet the countess!"

"B-but where am I?"

"At the countess's summer ball. At her estate. Just outside of Paris."

"Paris," Belle said, not daring to believe it. "I'm in a château on the edge of *Paris?*"

The young man bent his head to hers. "Of course! Isn't that what a good story does? It pulls you in and never lets you go."

69

He offered Belle his arm. "The *comtesse des Terres des Morts* wishes to meet you," he said. "And the countess is not one to be kept waiting."

Belle was taken aback by the countess's title. "Terres des Morts . . ." she echoed. "Land of the Dead? I'm not sure I wish to meet her!"

The young man laughed. "It's a horrible title, I agree. It was given to an ancestor of the countess's. After he'd won a particularly bloody battle. It is much fiercer than she is, I promise you."

Belle hesitated. "What *is* this place?" she asked.

"A bit of magic, like all good books," the man replied. "An escape. A place where you can leave cares and worries behind." He smiled. "At least for a chapter or two." He offered her his arm.

Belle bit her lip. She cast a glance behind her. It wasn't too late to leave. It wasn't too late to run out of the château, down the drive, through the portal, and back to the Beast's castle.

But there, she could only read stories. Here, it seemed, she could live one.

"I must return to the countess," the young man said, lowering his arm. "Turn *Nevermore's* pages if you wish, or close its cover. The choice is yours."

He bowed, then turned to leave.

"Wait!" Belle cried.

He turned back to her, a questioning look on his face. Belle looked into his beautiful eyes again. They sparkled with mystery and a hint of mischief.

Paris. A grand mansion. A mysterious countess. An elegant escort, she thought.

The story was off to a tantalizing start.

"Shall we?" the young man asked.

Belle took a deep breath. "Yes," she replied. "We shall."

CHAPTER TWELVE

"MY NAME IS HENRI, by the way," the young man said.

He squired her through the foyer and down a hallway filled with statues and paintings.

"Just Henri?" Belle inquired.

"You require my full title?" he asked with a roguish smile. "Very well, then. Henri, *duc des Choses-Passées*, at your service."

Belle blinked. It was not every day she attended a ball, on the outskirts of Paris, on the arm of a duke.

Henri raised an eyebrow at her silence. "Ah, I'm very sorry. I've disappointed you. You were hoping for a prince."

Belle recovered her voice. "I was not!" she protested.

"You were. Admit it. He would be dashing, handsome, and rich. Carrying a glass slipper, of course, and ready to marry you after a single dance."

Belle saw that he was teasing her. "You are *completely* ridiculous!" she said.

Henri, grinning now, swept his hand in an arc in front of them. "Picture it!" he said. "You'd live in a sumptuous palace, where you'd be waited on hand and foot by a hundred servants. You'd eat cake for breakfast and strudel for dinner, and you'd never get out of bed. You'd have monkeys, parrots, and hedgehogs."

"This is starting to sound tempting," said Belle, playing along. "I *do* love hedgehogs."

"You'd have beautiful little princes and princesses. Twenty of them."

Belle's eyebrows shot up. "Is that all?"

"Not enough? Thirty, then. You and your prince would lead marvelous lives—playing checkers, knitting socks, bestowing largesse on the peasants, ruling the world. . . ."

"All from our *bed?*"

"You'd have to put wheels on it, of course."

The image of a prince and princess ruling from a rolling bed was so absurd, Belle burst out laughing.

"You'd live happily ever after. On nothing but love and pastries. Isn't that how these stories go?"

"These stories, yes. Not mine," Belle said.

"No Prince Charming for you, then?" Henri asked. "No handsome knight to swoop in on a white horse and save you? I'm not surprised. I hear you're the type of girl who does the saving herself. You saved your father from life in a prison cell at the hands of a beast."

Belle stopped short. "How do you know that?" she asked, suddenly uncomfortable. Henri was witty and fun, but he was still a stranger.

Henri didn't answer. They'd come to a pair of open doors. Beyond them was a magnificent ballroom. An orchestra was playing. Guests were dancing a graceful minuet.

"Are you ready, Belle?" he asked.

"You know my name, too?" Belle asked apprehensively.

"The countess told me about you. She's very interested in you."

"She is? Why? How does *she* know me?"

But Henri's gaze was directed toward the ballroom.

"Come," he said. "It's time."

CHAPTER THIRTEEN

ON A RED DAMASK CHAIR that looked much like a throne, a woman, regal and straight-backed, was holding court.

Her raven hair was swept up and held in place with jet-black combs. A ruby choker circled her neck. A gown of black silk set off her pale skin and red lips. It was impossible to guess her age—no lines etched her face, but her eyes, as green as emeralds, were deeply wise.

Glances were traded as Henri and Belle approached her. Whispers were exchanged behind painted fans.

Henri swept a deep bow to the woman. As he straightened,

he said, "Madame Comtesse, allow me to present Mademoiselle Belle from *Château de la Bête*. Mademoiselle, the comtesse des Terres des Morts."

"It is an honor to meet you, Madame Comtesse," Belle said, curtsying.

She was eager to ask the countess a thousand questions but felt it would be awkward to do so in front of so many curious onlookers.

The countess's shrewd eyes appraised Belle. "The honor is mine, mademoiselle. I'm delighted you've joined us. There is much for us to talk about. . . ."

Music started to play, cutting her off. Belle recognized the opening notes of a dance called the passacaglia.

"My favorite!" the countess exclaimed. "We shall dance first, my dear girl, and chat later when we're both exhausted!"

As if on cue, a tall man, his chest festooned with medals, bowed to the countess, then led her to the dance floor.

Henri, following suit, offered Belle his hand, but Belle hesitated again, struck anew by a dizzying sense of unreality.

Henri gave her an encouraging smile. "Haven't you always said that you want more than a provincial life? It's not every day you find yourself in an exciting story. Make something of it, Belle."

On the dance floor, partners were lining up across from

each other, smiling and laughing. The color was high in their cheeks. The music grew louder, and more insistent. And Belle, unable to resist it, impulsively joined in.

The next few minutes sped by like a ride through the woods on a wild horse. The touch of hands and whirl of bodies, the stamp of heels on the floor—it was intoxicating. Belle's heart beat in time to the music. She felt light and free.

When the dance ended, Belle was winded. Henri led her to the edge of the dance floor so that she could catch her breath, and there he bumped into an acquaintance of his, an actor from London.

"Edward and his troupe are in Paris for a production of *Hamlet*," he explained after he introduced Edward to Belle.

"Really?" Belle said, excited to meet such a distinguished person. "I would love to see it. *Hamlet*'s one of Shakespeare's best plays, I think. Better than *Macbeth* and *Othello*."

Edward gave her a patronizing smile. "Oh? And what does a pretty girl know of Shakespeare? Let me guess. . . . 'To be, or not to be: that is the question'?" he drawled.

Belle winced at the man's rudeness. She'd met his kind before. Villeneuve had its share of self-important swaggerers, and she'd learned how to deal with them.

Smiling sweetly, she cleared her throat. "'Who's there?'" she intoned, in as deep a voice as she could muster.

Edward blinked at her. "I beg your pardon?" he said.

Belle cocked her head. "Surely you recognize the play's opening line, monsieur?" she said challengingly. "Why don't you take the next one? And then back and forth we'll go until one of us makes a mistake."

Excitement rippled through the crowd. "A contest!" whispered a woman. "A duel of words!" trilled another.

"Don't be silly. I'm a trained Shakespearean, a thespian of great renown. You'll only embarrass yourself," said Edward scornfully.

Henri's eyes twinkled with devilry. "Come, Belle," he said baitingly. "Monsieur Edward, it appears, is afraid of a dare."

Edward snorted. "That's absurd," he said. Then he turned to Belle. "When you lose and are crying in your handkerchief, mademoiselle, don't say I didn't warn you."

"I won't," Belle promised.

Edward took a deep, theatrical breath and blew it out again. He closed his eyes, touched his fingers to his temples, and in a booming voice said, "'Nay, answer me: stand, and unfold yourself!'"

"'Long live the king!'" Belle replied, grinning.

"Bernardo?"

"'He.'"

"'You come most carefully upon your hour.'"

"''Tis now struck twelve; get thee to bed, Francisco,'" said Belle, without missing a beat.

Edward's smug expression melted away. An anxious one took its place. The words flew fast and furious between them, each as true as a marksman's shot. The crowd pressed in, marveling as Edward and Belle shifted from line to line, and character to character, without so much as a stumble.

Scene One gave way to Scene Two. Sweat beaded on Edward's forehead. Color rose in Belle's cheeks. Her grin broadened. Her heart thrilled to the competition.

Hamlet was Pere Robert's favorite play. How many dull, rainy mornings and endless winter afternoons had the two of them spent reciting it? Sometimes Pere Robert would take the part of Hamlet, brandishing an old broom as a sword. Other times he was Gertrude with a dish rag on his head. Belle might be Ophelia one day, Laertes the next. She could recite the play in her sleep.

Scene Two shifted to Scene Three. Edward had just launched into Laertes's lecture to Ophelia on her conduct when he flubbed a line. Belle picked it up, finished the soliloquy, and curtsied. As she rose, the crowd burst into applause.

"*That*, monsieur," she said pertly, "is what a pretty girl knows about Shakespeare."

Edward gave her a stiff bow, gracelessly conceding defeat, and turned on his heel.

Henri was instantly at Belle's side. "Well done!" he said. "Serves him right, the pompous fool."

"Henri!" Belle scolded.

"Sorry, but it does! And he is!"

A jeweled maharaja approached Belle. He bowed, then asked her if she would be his partner for the next passacaglia. Belle danced with him, and kept dancing. She didn't sit down for a full hour. Minuets, allemandes, voltas—she was in demand for them all. During the short rests between songs, she mingled with painters and professors. Laughed with philosophers. She met a Yoruban prince, an explorer from Peru, a sculptor from Warsaw. The empress dowager of China invited her to the Forbidden City to visit the imperial palace.

And then, when she was finally completely out of breath, Belle felt an arm snake through hers.

"Have you worn holes in your slippers yet?" the countess asked her, her eyes bright with amusement.

Belle lifted her skirts and peered at her dancing slippers. Her big toes were poking through the delicate fabric. She dropped her skirts, blushing.

"Wonderful! That's the proof of a good ball!" the countess

declared, steering Belle toward a terrace. "Come, walk with me, child. I'm in need of fresh air."

She was fanning herself as she spoke, and her perfume wafted around her, spicy and rich. Belle was certain she'd smelled it before, but couldn't remember where.

A hulking servant with bright, beady eyes and a large hooked nose opened a set of French doors for them, bowing as his mistress passed. He was dressed in black livery with a ruff of white at his neck.

"I've heard so much about you, Belle," the countess said as they stepped out onto the terrace. "I know that you adore books, and that you wish to travel, and"—she paused and gave Belle a searching glance—"that your present situation is rather difficult. I do hope that the evening has lightened your heart a little."

"Pardon, my lady, but how do you know all these things?" Belle asked. "We've only just met." She felt the same, sudden twinge of discomfort she'd felt with Henri, when he'd told her things about herself a stranger couldn't possibly know.

The countess laughed. "This is *Paris*, child! Word travels. I know so many people, you see. I make the acquaintance of *everyone*, sooner or later. They all come through *Nevermore*."

"But what is *Nevermore*? How does all . . . all *this*," Belle gestured at the château, the guests, the twinkling lanterns, the graceful cherry trees. "How does it *happen?*"

The countess smiled coyly. "Why, through the magic of storytelling, of course. I'm *Nevermore's* author, you see. It's a special book. *Very* special. It contains many stories. But *this* story? Ah, Belle, *this* one I'm writing just for you."

"Why?" Belle asked. "Why *me?*"

But the countess didn't hear her question. She and Belle had strolled to the far edge of the terrace, and her attention had been captured by something there.

"Refreshments have been served. At last!" she said, pointing to a gorgeous display. "Let's see what my cooks have come up with. I'm famished!"

Tempting delicacies had been set out on tables draped with white linen and garlanded with roses and lilacs. Bottles of champagne stood in sterling wine coolers. A crystal bowl contained sparkling punch. Pastries were displayed on porcelain platters, and sugared fruit tumbled from footed stands.

The countess let go of Belle's arm. "Doesn't it look *divine?*" she said. "My baker is the best in Paris. Do help yourself."

Belle thought the macarons, arranged by color on a silver tray, looked delicious. She chose a chocolate one, bit into it, and rolled her eyes with pleasure.

Just as she was about to reach for a second, a fearsome

stag beetle landed smack in the center of them, hissing at her. Belle uttered a cry and snatched her hand away. The creature was as big as an apple, with a shiny black body, iridescent wings, and two spiky horns on its head.

Two more beetles were crawling over a raspberry tart, their spiky legs sinking into the custard filling. They'd plundered the tart of its berries and used them to spell out words on the white tablecloth. Leaning in as close as she dared, Belle read them.

THREE THINGS EATEN,

LOVE LIES BEATEN.

THREE THINGS LOST,

A DREADFUL COST.

The countess read them, too. Her eyes flashed with anger. "Filthy vermin!" she sputtered. She snapped her fan shut and tried to whack the beetles with it, but she missed and hit a stand of pastries instead. The stand went over, crashing into plates and platters. Pastries rolled off the table and splattered on the floor.

"Mouchard! Come!" the countess shouted.

The hulking servant in black immediately appeared.

"Kill them!" the countess ordered coldly. "Kill them *all.*"

Mouchard grabbed a silver serving spoon and hurried to comply with his mistress's command, but the clever beetles had already crawled down the table and were heading for the garden.

As Mouchard chased them, other servants cleaned up the mess. Fresh pastries were brought out.

"I'm so sorry, my dear," the countess said. "I hope you'll have some tart? A bit of cake?"

But Belle found that she'd lost her appetite. The insects had startled her, but worse, they'd unsettled her.

"I've never encountered beetles that can spell. Their message was so strange. I wonder what it means," she said.

"Nothing. It's gibberish," the countess replied tersely. "A madwoman keeps them. She lives nearby. On occasion the wretched things escape."

"A madwoman? *Here?*" Belle said, alarmed. "Is she part of the story?"

"I'm afraid so. She's part of everyone's story, unfortunately."

"Is she dangerous?" Belle asked, warily looking around.

"Highly," said the countess. "She's completely deranged. She has silvery blond hair and usually wears white. Avoid her at all costs."

"I will," Belle said, with a shiver.

A servant walked by bearing a fresh plate of macarons.

The countess took it from him. "Enough of unpleasant topics. Here, child, *do* have another sweet."

"Thank you, my lady, but I can't," Belle said. "I'm expected for dinner. I must be getting back."

Out here on the terrace, away from the music and dancing, Belle was becoming aware that time had passed. Mrs. Potts was readying a meal for her.

"I'm sorry to see you go, Belle. I enjoyed meeting you," the countess said.

"I enjoyed meeting you, too," said Belle. "Thank you for this magical ball. For allowing me to be part of *Nevermore*, if only for an evening."

"You can be part of *Nevermore* again, child. It's your story. Return to it whenever you wish," the countess said.

Then she gathered Belle into her arms and hugged her tightly. As she released her, one of her rings snagged in a tendril of Belle's hair, pulling out several long strands.

"Oh! Ow!" Belle said, wincing.

"My poor girl. I'm so sorry," said the countess.

"It's nothing," Belle assured her. "Please don't worry about it."

"Monsieur Henri will show you out," the countess said as the handsome young duke appeared.

As Belle and Henri walked away, the countess removed

the strands of Belle's hair from her ring and wrapped them around her finger. Her eyes glittered as she did, and her smile darkened.

Henri escorted Belle back through the mansion's front doors and down its steps, and then he walked her back up the long drive. The book was right where Belle had left it, near the gate, its pages still shimmering. All she had to do was step through it and she'd be back in the Beast's castle.

"I'm sorry you have to go," Henri said. "Did you enjoy your evening?"

"So much," Belle said.

"Then you'll come back?"

Was it an invitation or a demand? Belle couldn't decide, and Henri didn't give her time to.

"You have friends here. Remember that," he said. "I'm one of them."

"Thank you," said Belle. "Thank you for everything." Then, with a last good-bye, she stepped out of *Nevermore*.

She was through the shimmering pages so quickly, she didn't see Henri smile—or hear his voice as he whispered, "We'll be waiting for you."

CHAPTER FOURTEEN

"BELLE!" A VOICE SHOUTED from the library. "Belle, are you in here?"

It was Chip.

"Coming!" Belle shouted back. She looked down at herself, relieved to see that she was again wearing her blue work dress and her sturdy brown boots. Only seconds ago, she'd stepped out of *Nevermore*. As she had, the cover had slammed shut and the book had shrunk back to its normal size.

"Belle!"

Belle quickly picked the book up off the floor and placed it back on the table where she'd found it. She started for the door, but before she got to it, she heard a different voice.

It's a special book. Very special. It contains many stories. But this story? Ah, Belle, this one I'm writing just for you.

Belle whirled around. It felt as if the countess had been standing right behind her, her words a cold breath on Belle's neck. But no one was there.

Belle's eyes fell on *Nevermore* again. Without fully knowing why, she dashed back across the room and grabbed the book. Then she opened a drawer in the desk, shoved the book inside, and closed the drawer again.

"Belle, where *are* you?"

"I'm here, Chip!" she called out, hurrying from the workroom. Chip was waiting for her by the library's doors.

"Dinner's ready! I looked all over for you!"

Belle pointed behind her. "I was back there. In a workroom. I found . . ."

"What, Belle? You found what?" Chip asked.

A magical book, she almost said. But then she didn't.

"This!" she said, pulling a dust rag out of her pocket. "Come on, Chip. Let's go downstairs."

Chip zoomed ahead of her. He was out of the library and down the stairs in no time.

Belle lagged behind, feeling bad that she'd told him a fib. She hadn't meant to. The words had just popped out of her mouth before she could stop them.

Now she realized why: because she didn't want to share the book.

Turn Nevermore's *pages if you wish, or close its cover. The choice is yours,* Henri had said.

The last choice Belle had made all on her own was to trade her freedom for her father's. It had been a hard and irrevocable one, and had made her a captive in the Beast's castle. Even before that fateful day, life in Villeneuve had offered her few choices. But now this enchanted book had appeared, filled with fascinating people. The decision to return to it—or not—was hers and hers alone, and she wanted to keep it that way.

"Belle, come *on!*"

Chip was bellowing for her from the bottom of the stairs now. "Cuisinier made tomato soup and toasted cheese sandwiches! They're going to get cold!" he yelled.

Belle's stomach growled. Toasted cheese sandwiches were her favorite, and it had been hours since she'd eaten. She found that in addition to being hungry, she was sore and weary. It had been a long day.

"I'll be right there!" she shouted.

She pulled the heavy library doors closed behind her and hurried down the stairs, looking forward to the warmth of the kitchen, to company and conversation, and to dinner.

Nevermore was, for the moment, forgotten. It lay in the desk drawer, in the small, dusty room. In the darkness.

But had anyone been standing in the room, near the desk, they might've smelled the scent of roses.

And heard a woman laughing.

CHAPTER FIFTEEN

ALONE IN HIS STUDY, long after his dinner had been brought to him and cleared away again, the Beast sat at his desk and recalled each moment that he had gotten to spend with Belle.

He pictured her at breakfast, her eyes bright and attentive, keen to get on with the day's activities. And later, in the library, disheveled, a coil of hair fallen out of her bun, trying not to laugh at his clumsy antics. He remembered her reciting lines from *The Faerie Queene* with him in her beautiful voice, a voice that lifted him out of himself and his accursed castle to a world where he was a good and noble prince—not a hideous beast.

Each of these scenes was a lovely tableau he felt lucky to have experienced, and thinking of them now made his heart quicken and brought a smile to his lips. He tried his best to simply savor these memories, but each one succumbed to a creeping regret that darkened it like a stormy sky.

His brief moment of happiness shattered as he glanced around the gloomy study. He couldn't help feeling that the broken pieces of his world were solely his fault.

His selfishness and arrogance had caused all of this. As he looked at the wilting rose on top of his broad desk, the joy he'd felt only moments ago disappeared. A familiar, piercing anguish took its place.

There was a knock at the door. It was Lumiere. The Beast bade him enter.

"Is there anything else you require tonight before retiring, master?"

"I—I thought we might go skating tomorrow."

Lumiere's eyebrows shot up. "Skating, master? *You?* You've never skated in your life!"

"Belle mentioned that she has skated before. Back in her village. I thought she might like to try it here. How hard can it be?"

"On the backside? Very," said Lumiere. "Nonetheless, I shall arrange it. Anything else?"

"No," said the Beast. Then, haltingly, "Thank you, Lumiere. For asking."

"Of course," said Lumiere, with a bow. "Good night, master."

He left the room, pulling the door closed behind him. Just as it was about to click shut, the Beast called out to him. "Lumiere . . . wait!"

"Master?" he said, opening the door again.

"Actually, there *is* something else . . ." the Beast began awkwardly.

"A cup of warm milk, perhaps?"

"Is Belle happy? Is she comfortable? The library—is she enjoying the library?" the Beast asked, all in a rush.

"Enjoying it?" Lumiere said, laughing. "I believe she'd move her bed into it if she could."

"Did you see her today?" asked the Beast. "Smiling when I tried to clean a window. Laughing when I decided to wear the mop bucket on my head." He shook his head, still mortified at the memory, but a small grin tugged at the corners of his mouth. "You've become her friends. She likes your company."

"It was *you* who delighted her today, master," Lumiere pointed out.

The Beast looked away. "How I've longed to hear those

93

words. I'd started to think I never would." His eyes sought Lumiere's. "Do you think she would ever be my friend? Has she softened toward me at all?"

Lumiere thought before answering. "Well, you *were* a terribly funny sight today," he said at length, underscoring the fact that anyone—fond of the Beast or not—would have laughed at the pandemonium in the library.

"Which is a tactful way of saying she hasn't," the Beast said, his heart sinking.

"These things happen slowly. Perhaps in time, master," said Lumiere.

"Something we have very little of," sighed the Beast, glancing at the rose. In the dim candlelight, it looked more fragile than ever.

"Very little," Lumiere agreed. He tried his best to muster a brave smile, but his efforts couldn't mask the toll the enchantment was taking on him.

In the early days, Lumiere's human form had shone through his candlestick body, particularly in moments like this. But his humanity was diminishing further every day. His movements were becoming stiff, his flames dim.

The Beast rarely admitted it, but he cared a great deal for Lumiere and the rest of his servants. He was watching them fade away into inanimate objects—imprisoned, in their own way, just like Belle—and it was all his fault.

He was the one who'd brought the terrible enchantment on himself, his servants, and his castle. And he was the one who would have to undo it—if he could.

With deep remorse, the Beast remembered the beggar woman who'd come to his castle the night of the ball, how she'd asked for his help and offered him a rose in return. How he'd laughed at her.

His eyes were still fixed on that same rose, under its glass cloche. The Enchantress had put it there, declaring that her curse could only be broken if he learned to love and was loved in return—by the time the last petal fell. If he did not, he would stay a beast forever, and those he'd doomed to suffer with him would die.

Many petals had fallen from the rose, but a few still remained.

"Do you think Belle will discover how the curse can be broken?" Lumiere asked, following the Beast's gaze.

"She hasn't guessed the truth yet, and we can't tell her. The Enchantress forbade it."

"I wish we *could* tell her," Lumiere said with a sigh. "It would certainly make things easier."

The Beast gently touched the glass protecting the rose. "Even if we could, what good would it do?" he asked, his voice heavy with sadness. "Look at me, Lumiere. Belle could never love me. She could only ever pity me."

"That is *not* true," Lumiere said. "Love—real love—sees with the heart, master. Not with the eyes."

The Beast looked at him skeptically. "How do you know that?"

"Because I'm in love with a woman who's a feather duster," said Lumiere. "*That's* how."

"I don't understand."

"No, you don't. But I hope you will one day. You deserve that. Everyone deserves that."

The Beast gave him a quizzical look. "Everyone deserves to fall in love with a feather duster?"

Lumiere chuckled. "Show Belle who you are, master. Who you *really* are. Show her your heart."

And then he bade the Beast good night.

Alone again, the Beast turned back to his desk, struggling with the riot of emotions their conversation had unleashed.

He'd suffer the consequences of the Enchantress's curse if he could trade himself for Lumiere and the other servants. Freeing Belle would shatter their only chance of ever becoming human again.

Long ago, in the early days of his enchantment, the Beast had grieved for himself and for all that he'd lost. Now, he grieved for others. His servants weren't the ones who'd been arrogant and cruel, yet they were paying the price. And Chip, little Chip. He was only a boy. Would his life end before it had even begun?

The Beast groaned. He gazed at the rose once more and its frail, tenuous beauty that still shone amidst such darkness. He moved closer, searching for something in its radiance. A bit of solace, perhaps. Of forgiveness. Of hope.

Another petal fell.

CHAPTER SIXTEEN

"OH!" GASPED BELLE, grabbing the Beast's arm as a mottled bird erupted from the snowy brush ahead of them, its wings beating the air.

"It's only a quail," the Beast said, smiling. He patted her hand, which she quickly withdrew, a bit embarrassed to have been startled so badly by a bird.

"There's nothing on these grounds you need to fear," the Beast continued. "At least in the daytime, when the wolves stay well in the woods."

Belle remembered the Beast fighting off an entire pack of wolves, and she couldn't help imagining that she'd be safe with him at any time of the day or night—anywhere.

The wintry outing had been the Beast's idea. He'd come downstairs after breakfast, announced that he was in need of some exercise, and asked Belle if she'd like to accompany him on a walk to the pond. Belle had jumped at the chance.

"We don't have much farther to go," the Beast said now, as they clambered over a stone wall.

Belle paused on top of the wall for a few seconds and took in the scene around her. It was breathtaking: a bleak winter landscape, but starkly beautiful, too. And despite the barren fields, the leafless oaks and snow-choked grasses, it was so full of life. Just this morning, she'd seen a falcon and two hawks in addition to the quail. There'd also been a red fox chasing a hare across the far field, and a lustrous mink poking around an icy brook.

"You seem lost in thought," the Beast said, snapping her out of her reverie. "You must have found a good book in the library."

His words startled Belle. She knew he couldn't be talking about *Nevermore* . . . could he?

"I-I did." She smiled, quickly recovering. "In fact, I found several hundred."

The Beast laughed, and Belle decided that there was no

way he knew about the comtesse des Terres des Morts's magical book. She'd been careful to put it well out of sight. It was curious to her how possessive she'd become of it.

"Are you going to stay up there all day?" the Beast asked.

"Quite possibly," Belle said. "The view is lovely from here."

"Hmm. That would be a shame. You'd miss seeing the pond, which is even lovelier."

Belle was about to climb down when she scented something in the air.

"Do you smell smoke?"

"I think I do."

It couldn't be coming from any of the castle's fireplaces, Belle reasoned. *We're too far away.*

She sniffed the air again. "And *chocolate?*"

"Is *that* what that is?" the Beast said, his eyes twinkling with mischief.

Belle looked down at him suspiciously. "What's going on?"

The Beast grinned. "Come down and I'll show you!" he said, holding out his paw.

Belle took it and jumped off the wall.

As soon as she was on the ground, the Beast released her hand and loped off.

"Slow down!" Belle shouted. "I can't run as fast as you!"

"Good!" the Beast called over his shoulder. "That means more chocolate for *me!*"

"Oh, you *cheater!*" Belle cried, tearing after him, her blue cloak flaring out behind her.

"All right, I'll slow down," the Beast said. He turned around and ran backward, and still Belle couldn't catch up with him. He made a face at her. Crossed his eyes, stuck his tongue out.

Belle stopped. She laughed in disbelief.

The Beast, too busy clowning to pay attention to his surroundings, didn't see the downed tree limb behind him, half-buried in the snow.

He tripped over it, went flying, and landed with a whump in a deep drift.

Belle burst into laughter. She couldn't stop. She laughed so hard she had to wipe tears out of her eyes.

Will he get angry again? she wondered. *Or has he learned to laugh at himself?*

She soon had her answer.

The Beast sat up. He shook the snow off his head. "I *meant* to do that," he said, with a grin.

"Of course you did," said Belle. She broke into a run again and sped past him. She could see the frozen pond in the distance through a line of trees.

"I'm *letting* you win, you know!" he called after her.

"Ha!" she called back.

She kept on running, across the field, through the trees, their bare-branched limbs a web of black against the gray sky. The ground crested as she neared the water, then dipped down.

As Belle reached the crest, she saw what had scented the air so deliciously.

A smile lit up her face.

With a cry of delight, she sped down the hill.

CHAPTER SEVENTEEN

AT THE EDGE OF THE FROZEN POND, a fire crackled in a big iron brazier.

Next to it stood two chairs fitted with cushions and draped with thick woolen throws. The pond had been shoveled free of snow. Three familiar figures were busy setting a small, collapsible table with a steaming pot of hot chocolate, cups and saucers, and a platter of beignets. A basket rested on the ground near the table.

Belle called to them. "Lumiere! Cogsworth! Chapeau!"

Chapeau waved.

Lumiere smiled.

Cogsworth complained. "The cold is wreaking havoc on

my gears," he moaned. "Everything has seized up. I'm five minutes slow already!"

"What are you doing out here?" Belle asked.

"Come and see!" Lumiere said, pointing at the basket on the ground. Belle ran over to it and peered inside. It contained two pairs of ice skates.

"You told me you liked to skate," the Beast said, coming up behind her.

"I do! Oh, thank you!" Belle said.

She was so touched by this unexpected thoughtfulness that she threw her arms around him. Slowly, uncertainly, as if he were afraid he might break her, the Beast put his arms around Belle and hugged her back.

Belle released him, grabbed the smaller pair of skates, and sat down in a chair. The skates were made of wood with leather straps and fitted with sharp steel blades that curved up at the toes. Belle fastened them over her boots and stood up.

"The ice is as smooth as glass," said Lumiere. "It's a perfect surface for skating."

"That reminds me . . ." said Cogsworth, stoking the fire. "Did I ever tell you about the time General Montgomery and I brought our cavalry across the frozen Saint Lawrence at the Battle of Quebec?"

Belle, smiling, rolled her eyes at Cogsworth's story and took that opportunity to whoosh off across the pond.

The Beast slowly minced his way out onto the ice. Once clear of the verge, he stopped—or tried to. His feet swept him swiftly forward and upward, and his body slammed down, right onto his backside. He got up, then fell again. And then again.

"Perhaps you should let me help you!" Belle called from across the pond, where she was cutting a graceful arc on the ice.

"Master, perhaps we should tie a pillow to your backside!" Cogsworth shouted fretfully from the shore.

The Beast turned and glared at him.

Belle quickly arrived and took the Beast's paws in her mittened hands. Skating slowly backward, she coaxed him forward. Her touch calmed him, she could tell, and his desire to move toward her propelled him.

Eventually, he was sliding alongside Belle and holding her hand well past the time he needed to. Around and around they skated, talking and laughing, Belle's cheeks pink, her eyes sparkling. The Beast forgot his apprehension toward the ice; his steps became smooth and confident. He glided farther with each one.

Winded, they stopped to enjoy the hot chocolate and

beignets. Then they skated some more. Minutes became hours, and the hours soon brought dusk.

"It's not wise to stay out much longer," the Beast said as the setting sun poked its last bits of golden light through the trees. "We need to be back in the castle, safe and sound, before dark."

Reluctantly, Belle and the Beast headed home, accompanied by the servants.

"I never did finish my story," Cogsworth announced on the way. "About Montgomery and Quebec. Shall I tell it now?"

The Beast shot Belle a dire glance. Belle bit her lip. Chapeau grimaced.

"Go ahead," said Lumiere absently. "It will make the time drag by."

Cogsworth gave him a look. "I believe you mean *speed* by."

"Do I? Er, I mean, I do!" Lumiere hastily amended.

When they finally arrived back at the castle, Mrs. Potts was at the door to greet them. She ushered them inside, where the overeager Chapeau took Belle's cloak—before she was entirely out of it.

She spun around to free her arm and crashed into the Beast, who reached out to catch her. They both laughed, and they looked into each other's eyes.

"Thank you," she said. "For a truly wonderful day."

"Come, child," Mrs. Potts interrupted, bustling Belle off toward the stairs. "You've been out in the cold air for hours! You need a hot bath to chase the chill from your bones."

As they headed up to Belle's room, talking a mile a minute about the day, Belle cast a glance back over her shoulder. But she was too far up the stairs to see the Beast, still standing in the foyer, as motionless as a statue, a wistful smile spreading across his face.

CHAPTER EIGHTEEN

"TELL ME A STORY, BELLE!"

"Chip, you should be asleep by now," Belle scolded, tucking the little teacup onto his shelf in the china cupboard.

It was getting late, and Mrs. Potts still had a good many chores to do. She'd asked Belle if she would put Chip to bed.

"*Please* tell me a story?"

Belle gave in. It was impossible to say no to that sweet little face. "All right. What kind of story?"

"No fairy tales. Something different," said Chip. "Tell me something *real*. Tell me about your village. What's it like?"

Belle cocked her head. "Villeneuve? It's a small place. It has a square, a market, and a fountain, just like every other village. A church with a tiny collection of books. It's quiet. But pretty," she said, surprised to find herself praising Villeneuve—and missing it a little. When she had lived there, all she'd wanted was to get away from it. "Everyone knows everyone, which is sometimes good . . . and sometimes *not* so good," she added with a laugh.

"What kind of people live there?" asked Chip.

"Well, there's Pere Robert, a learned man who's the village's curé and its librarian. And of course there's my father. His name is Maurice. He makes the most beautiful music boxes you've ever seen. He's smart. He truly has the soul of an artist. . . ." She smiled. "And he's kind. So kind." Belle's heart knotted, as it always did when she talked about her father, or even thought of him. Tears stung behind her eyes. She had to look away for a second to collect herself.

Chip noticed her sadness. "You must miss him."

Belle nodded. "Very much."

"I'm sorry, Belle."

"Me too, Chip." Determined not to cry, she changed the subject. "There's also a flower seller who always has the most beautiful blooms. A fishwife with a sharp tongue. A baker. A greengrocer. And . . ." Belle made a face. "*Gaston.*"

Chip giggled. "Who's that?"

"God's gift to women."

"Really?"

"He certainly thinks so."

"It doesn't sound like you miss *him* very much."

"Not at all," Belle said. "There is someone else I miss, though—Agathe."

"Who is she?"

"The bravest person I know."

"What did she do?" Chip asked, wide-eyed. "Fight off robbers? Pirates?"

"I'll tell you, and then it's lights out. Do we have a deal?"

"Deal!" Chip said.

"We had a neighbor in Villeneuve. His name was Rémi," Belle began. "When I was small, he lost his little boy to a terrible fever. He went crazy with grief. His hair grew long. He became thin and dirty. Pain turned his eyes dark and wild."

"He sounds scary," Chip said, with a shiver.

"He was," said Belle. "He pushed everyone away, snarling if a friend or neighbor came too close. His wife left him. His parents could not get near him. One by one, the villagers turned their backs on him. Only Agathe refused to give up."

"Who was she?"

"A beggar woman known to everyone in the village. People were in the square one day—it was a market day—talking about Rémi. Most were not saying nice things, and Agathe got fed up with them. She rarely talked to anyone in town, but she spoke up on this day.

" 'Rémi has always been kind to me,' she said. 'He gave me food. He offered me shelter. I will speak with him.' But everyone begged her not to," Belle explained.

" 'He's too unpredictable!' said the mayor.

" 'He's a wild animal!' said the baker.

" 'He'll hurt you, foolish woman,' said Gaston. 'Let's shoot him and be done.'

"And do you know what she told them?"

"What?" said Chip.

" 'Love is not for cowards.' "

Chip nodded, digesting this.

"Agathe begged a bit of cheese and a loaf of bread from a shopkeeper, then walked to Rémi's house. I followed her as far as the gate, watching as she entered his yard. The second he saw her, he rushed at her with a pitchfork. 'Go!' he shouted. 'Get out of here!' I was so scared for her."

"What did you do?" asked Chip.

"I begged her to come back, but she paid me no attention. She went right up to Rémi and said, 'Your son was kind and good. Is this how you honor his memory?' "

"Rémi stopped dead. He threw his pitchfork to the

ground. 'My son!' he cried. 'My boy . . . my little boy! Death has taken him from me!'

"His legs gave way and he sank to the ground, helpless in his despair. Agathe sat down next to him. She gave him the bread and cheese she'd brought and made him eat them.

"'Listen to me, Rémi,' she said. 'Death wins only if you let her.'

"Rémi shook his head. Tears rolled down his cheeks. 'How can I defeat death, Agathe?' he asked. 'I cannot bestow life. I am not God.'

"Agathe laughed. 'You think *life* is the vanquisher of death? It is not. *Love* is. Life is fragile. Life ends. But love? Love lives forever,' she told him.

"Rémi wept then, like a child. From that day, little by little, he returned to us. Love brought him back."

Chip was quiet for a bit. Then he said, "You're right, Belle. Agathe *is* brave."

"Very," Belle agreed. She leaned into the cupboard and kissed him. "And now it's time for bed. Good night, Chip."

She started to shut the cupboard door, but as she did, Chip piped up again. "Belle?"

"Go to *sleep*," Belle scolded.

"He's just like Rémi."

"Who is?"

"The master. He's the way he is because he's hurting, too."

Belle paused, amazed by the child's perceptiveness. "Do you want to know something, Chip?" she asked.

Chip nodded.

"You would like Agathe. Very much. And she would like you."

Chip smiled, then closed his eyes. And Belle closed the cupboard door. She bade Mrs. Potts good night, lit a candle, and left the kitchen. She was tired after skating all day and ready for her own bed.

She walked along the main hallway to the stairs. The castle always seemed darker and more forlorn to her at this time of night. She knew that other smaller hallways branched off the main one. She'd explored some of the rooms they led to. In one sat a desk upon which lay invitations—sealed and addressed, but never sent. In another, fine silver and china were tucked away in cabinets for parties that never happened. She'd discovered the most beautiful dresses packed in trunks. A rocking horse with a little leather saddle. A small bow and quiver.

An air of ruin hung over the castle always. Tonight, though, it seemed heavier than ever.

This place could use an Agathe of its own, Belle thought.

She remembered the way Rémi had looked when Agathe

approached him. She remembered his eyes, so full of pain. She'd seen the same pain in the Beast's eyes. He was better at hiding it than Rémi had been, but in unguarded moments it surfaced.

Belle wondered if he would ever talk about it. The desire to know more about him, and to find out why she was here, was still strong inside her, but she shuddered as she recalled what had happened the last time she'd tried to find things out—the shouting and raging in the West Wing, her wild ride through the woods, the wolves.

She and the Beast had spent more time together since that terrible night. He'd given her the amazing gift of his library. They'd gone skating. They'd gotten to know each other a bit. Maybe trust each other a bit, too.

But was there enough trust for him to talk about the painful past?

Would she ever get the chance?

Belle didn't know.

She came to the stairway that led to the upper floors of the castle and her bedroom, and as she climbed it, she wondered if she could ever be as brave as Agathe.

CHAPTER NINETEEN

BELLE PUNCHED HER PILLOW.

She fluffed it, kneaded it, plumped it, and—finally—laid her head back down on it.

But it was no use. She couldn't fall asleep again.

Sighing, she rolled onto her side. From this position, she could see the row of windows on the far wall of her room and the moon, so solitary and remote, shining in the night sky. She wondered if it felt as lonely as she did.

She knew what had caused her loneliness—telling Chip about Villeneuve. Agathe. Pere Robert.

And most of all, her beloved father, Maurice.

Belle always tried her best not to think of him. It was too

painful. But tonight, no matter how hard she tried to push them away, memories of him, and of their happy life together, flooded her heart.

She cherished those memories, because in them, she and her father were together again. But they tortured her, too, for they underscored something she could barely bring herself to accept: that she would never, ever see him again.

Belle had made a deal—a dark, dreadful bargain—and now she had to keep it.

All because her father had picked a rose from the Beast's garden.

For her.

"Why didn't I ask for a daisy? A sunflower? A carnation?" she whispered, filled with regret. "If only I had, I wouldn't be here."

She remembered the day she'd lost him so clearly.

He'd gone to a market in a neighboring town to sell some of the beautiful music boxes he made.

Constructed to look like castles, cathedrals, and palaces, each music box was unique and involved hours of painstaking work. She recalled the care he'd taken in gilding a miniature Versailles with a paintbrush and magnifying glass, or shaping the stained-glass windows of a tiny Notre Dame with a diamond-tipped cutter.

"What would you like me to bring you?" he'd asked Belle as he'd set off, his wagon hitched to Philippe.

"Only a rose, Papa," she'd replied, well aware that they did not have money to spend on presents.

She'd been hanging out the wash when Philippe had returned home without the wagon—or her father.

"Take me to him," she'd said to the horse, terrified that her father had been in an accident or been set upon by robbers.

Philippe had taken her through the woods to an ancient castle, deep within a dark forest. She'd dismounted in the castle's keep, calling out to whoever owned it, but no one answered her. Bravely, she entered the castle and searched for her father. She finally found him—imprisoned in a tower.

"Papa!" she cried out when she saw him, thrusting her hand through the bars of his cell.

"Belle? Is that you?" he'd said, clasping it. "How did you find me? Belle, you must leave here at once. This castle is alive! Now go, before he finds you!"

Just then, the Beast appeared to Belle, shouting and raging. Belle had been frightened at first, but then she'd stood up to him and demanded that he release her father. When the Beast refused, she'd offered to take her father's place. Maurice was clearly ill, and Belle promised him that she'd find a way to escape. But she knew that she couldn't leave him trapped in that tower.

The Beast had granted her request, and Maurice had been released. That was the last Belle had seen of him. A hundred times a day she thought about him, despite her best efforts. Worried about him. Missed him. They'd always had each other, but he was alone now. Who would look after him? Who would make his morning coffee just the way he liked it? Who would see to it that he wore his woolen muffler when the weather turned cold?

Tears threatened again, just as they had when she'd told Chip his bedtime story.

Desperate to distract herself, Belle sat up in her bed and threw back the covers. She slid her feet into a pair of warm slippers, then shrugged into her woolen robe and walked to the windows.

Lacy swirls of frost framed the glass panes. It had snowed after she and the Beast had come in from skating, and a thick blanket of white glittered in the moonlight. As she gazed out at the wintry night, the enormous grandfather clock downstairs began to strike the hour, its deep, doleful chime echoing throughout the castle.

"Midnight," Belle said when it finished. "I have to get some sleep."

She looked at her bed without much hope, though, knowing full well that she would only toss and turn if she got back in it.

Back at home, when she couldn't sleep, her father had always made her a warm drink and let her read by candlelight until sleep stole over her.

A cup of hot milk would be just the thing, she thought. *That and a good book.*

She lit the candle on her bedside table by holding its wick to the glowing coals in her fireplace, then left her room, taking care to step quietly so that she wouldn't wake anyone.

Coals were still glowing in the kitchen's hearth, too. They threw off a welcoming warmth. A cast-iron pot containing the morning's oatmeal had been hung over them to cook slowly overnight. A large bowl of bread dough, covered with a cloth, had been set on the wooden table to rise. Baskets of apples, pears, and quince sat next to them, ready to be made into pies and compotes.

Belle loved the coziness of the kitchen. It was her second-favorite room in the castle, after the library. Cuisinier was sound asleep and she didn't want to wake him, so she heated milk in a small pot over the coals. Careful not to disturb Chip and Mrs. Potts, she got a mug, poured in the hot milk, and added a spoonful of honey. After she washed the pot and put it away, she made her way to the library, her mug in one hand, her candle in the other.

It was cold and dark there, but wood and kindling had been laid in the fireplace. Belle lit the kindling with her candle, and a few minutes later, she had a cheerful fire blazing. Two comfortable chairs faced each other across the hearth. A low table stood between them. It made a very inviting reading nook.

"All I need now is a book," Belle said.

She wished she could visit *Nevermore* but was unsure if the book's time followed real time. It wouldn't do to knock on the countess's door in the middle of the night.

Picking up her candle once more, Belle made her way down a row of bookcases—and nearly stumbled over a book that lay open on the floor. She bent down to peer at it. *Fearsome Pirates of the High Seas*, the title read. Perrault's *Tales of Times Past* and an edition of *Aesop's Fables* lay next to it.

"*Chip,*" Belle said, shaking her head. Like most children, he was good at taking things out, but not so good at putting them away again.

Belle reshelved the pirate book and Perrault's fairy tales. She was just about to put the book of fables away, too, when she paused instead, captivated by its beautiful cover. It showed a picture of a lion holding out its bloodied paw. A man stood nearby, reaching his hand out to the suffering creature.

"Androcles," she murmured. The story of the runaway slave and the lion he helped was one of her favorite fables. Her father had often read it to her.

Her eyes roved over the picture, taking in Androcles's brave expression and the lion's agonized one, and as they did, Chip's words came back to her. *He's the way he is because he's hurting, too.*

"Just like the lion," Belle whispered. "Chip, you're a *genius*."

She stood up, excitement coursing through her. She'd just come up with a way to draw the Beast out, to get him to talk to her, maybe even answer her questions.

Sometimes words alone were not enough, because they spoke only to the head. But a *story*, one in which the words were strung together as beautifully as pearls on a necklace . . . *that* would speak to the heart. And if Belle could speak to the Beast's heart, maybe she could get him to open it.

Belle carried the book back to the fireplace, intending to reread it. She had a plan now. She would find the Beast tomorrow—that would give her plenty of time to work up her nerve—and she would ask him if he'd ever heard the story of Androcles.

But as Belle neared the hearth, she saw she wouldn't have to wait until tomorrow to put her plan in action.

For the Beast was standing in the doorway in his dressing gown, a candleholder in his paw and a worried expression on his face.

CHAPTER TWENTY

"IT'S *YOU*, BELLE! I should've known," the Beast said, the concern on his face softening into relief.

"What's the matter?" Belle asked.

"Nothing, now," he said. "I smelled smoke and wanted to make sure nothing was out of sorts."

"I couldn't sleep, so I decided to get a hot drink and read." Belle gestured at the crackling fire. "Would you like to join me?"

The Beast nodded, and they both sat down in front of the fireplace.

"I'm surprised you're up. I thought you'd be snoring like a sailor—"

"Why, thank you."

"—after all the skating you did today. Why can't you sleep?"

"Something woke me. An owl, I think," she fibbed. She didn't want to tell him the truth. About being lonely, and missing her father.

But the Beast saw through the fib. "Belle, I know this is not what you wanted," he said, looking down at his paws. "Is there anything else we can do for you?"

Belle put her mug down. Butterflies were fluttering in her stomach. Steeling herself for an angry reaction, she said, "Yes, there is. My life changed forever. All because of a single rose. I want you to tell me why."

The Beast sat back in his chair. His eyes went to the fire. "Roses have thorns, and thorns leave wounds."

He spoke the words so quietly that Belle wasn't even sure he had meant for her to hear them. But she had, and she sensed a deep sorrow in them. It caught her completely off guard. She'd been prepared for roaring and snarling, not soft-spoken sadness.

"Wounds can heal if you pull the thorns out," she said.

"For some, perhaps," said the Beast.

It's now or never, Belle thought. She plunged ahead.

"Have you ever heard the tale of Androcles and the lion?" she asked, holding up the copy of *Aesop's Fables*.

The Beast shook his head. He looked cornered. "Belle, don't," he said.

But Belle didn't listen. She got out of her chair, knelt by his leg, and began her tale.

"A long time ago, there was a slave named Androcles. His master was very cruel, so Androcles ran away. When night fell, he took shelter in a cave, tired and hungry. But the cave was a lion's den, and the lion was in it. He came out of the shadows, growling and baring his teeth."

As Belle spoke, she took one of the Beast's paws into her hands.

"Poor Androcles!" she exclaimed. "Terrified, he cowered against a wall, certain he was about to die. But then, just as he thought all was lost . . . the lion held out his paw."

Slowly, Belle uncurled the Beast's own knotted paw.

"Androcles saw that the paw was bloody and swollen," she said. "Shoring up his courage, he approached the lion. A thorn was stuck in the pad. Ever so gently, Androcles pulled it out. The lion was grateful and helped Androcles in turn by hunting food for him. A few days later, though, Androcles was captured. He was thrown in prison, and eventually he was made to fight wild animals in an arena for the emperor's pleasure—"

"And one of those wild animals was the very lion Androcles had helped," the Beast cut in, a bitter note in his voice. "The creature recognized him and lay down at Androcles's feet. The emperor was so amazed, he granted Androcles his freedom, and they all lived happily ever after. Like people in fairy tales do. But life isn't a fairy tale, Belle."

"Actually, neither is the story of Androcles," said Belle. "It's a fable. It has a moral to it. A point. About how friends help each other."

The Beast withdrew his paw from Belle's hands. "And your telling it to me . . . does *that* have a point?"

"Yes, it does. You are like that lion. There's a thorn lodged deeply in you. It pains you greatly and causes you to—"

The Beast shot to his feet so abruptly, he knocked his chair over. It hit the floor with a booming crash, making Belle flinch.

"Be careful, Belle. Not all who try to befriend lions succeed," he said, his fur bristling.

Belle saw that she'd cut close to the bone. She sensed the Beast's rising anger, but she didn't back away from it. She was angry herself. She was trying so hard, and the Beast wasn't trying at all.

"What are you going to do?" she asked, standing up. "Roar at me again? Snarl and snap, like you did when I went to the West Wing?"

"No, I'm going to *leave*. Because I'm finished with this discussion. Finished with silly stories and even sillier metaphors," he said, starting toward the door.

But Belle ran ahead of him. "No more metaphors. No more symbols or similes," she said, blocking the door. "What aren't you telling me? I know there must be more to this curse than you or anyone will say. If I am to live out the rest of my days here, I deserve to know the truth, don't I?"

The Beast stopped. A low growl came from his throat. It unnerved her. She'd seen his rage before. She knew it was like a living thing—a cruel, malicious demon.

Stop, a voice inside her head said. *Don't push him any further. You don't know what he'll do.*

But Belle ignored it.

"I know about your childhood. I know about the ball and the Enchantress. I know what happened to you. But that doesn't mean you have to live your life this way."

The Beast's eyes narrowed. His ears flattened against his head. "I believe I have a better question: why did your father come here? Why did you? I didn't ask him to. I didn't ask you to. I didn't ask for *any* of this!" he shouted.

"And I *did*?" Belle shouted back.

The Beast clenched his paws. He looked away. "You don't *know*, Belle. You don't even know what you're asking," he said.

"Then tell me," she said plaintively. *"Please."*

The Beast raised his eyes to hers, and the pain Belle saw in their blue depths was so profound, it pierced her heart.

"I would tell you everything if I could, Belle," he said brokenly. "I'd give you the answers to your questions, the keys to this cursed castle, the secrets of my heart. But I can't. Please understand. I *can't.*"

And then he was gone.

Through the doorway. Out of the library.

And Belle was alone.

Once again.

CHAPTER TWENTY-ONE

BELLE STARED AT THE EMPTY DOORWAY, her heart aching.

For the Beast. For herself.

She'd thought he might roar and rage, but he hadn't, and his sadness was even worse than his anger.

With a heavy sigh, she sat back down in front of the fire.

She'd tried, again. And she'd failed, again. The Beast would not, or could not, give her the answers she wanted.

She picked up *Aesop's Fables*, thinking she might as well try to read it, but soon found she had no heart for it. Her drink had grown cold. The fire was burning down.

I should go back to bed, she thought.

Belle banked the fire. She would bring her mug down to the kitchen in the morning. She headed toward the window seat where she'd found *Aesop's Fables* to put the book away—and that's when she heard it: laughter, low and throaty.

It was coming from the back of the library.

From Nevermore, Belle thought.

The laughter continued, reminding Belle of the countess's elegant mansion, the glittering ball, and the princes, maharajas, and sultans she'd danced with.

It was late, but perhaps the countess was up. That was her laughter, wasn't it? Perhaps Belle could visit her.

She wouldn't be alone in *Nevermore*. She wouldn't be sad. There would be the countess to talk with. And Henri.

His words came back to her now. *You have friends here. Remember that. I'm one of them.*

Friends, Belle thought. *People with whom I can share things. People who open their hearts instead of locking them away.*

Belle rose and started toward the workroom, where *Nevermore* lay tucked away.

She would live out her days here in the Beast's castle, which was cruel enough—with no idea why, which was even crueler.

But *Nevermore* could provide her with a wonderful escape from her sorrows. For a few hours, she could find distraction in its lovely pages. Solace. Comfort. For a few hours, she could forget.

Belle's steps quickened. Her slippers scuffed softly over the library's wooden floor.

By the time she reached the workroom door, she was running.

CHAPTER TWENTY-TWO

"BELLE, MY DARLING GIRL! You've come back!" the countess exclaimed, delighted.

She was sitting in an open-topped phaeton in front of her mansion. Four black stallions, snorting and pawing, were harnessed to the graceful carriage. Lamps blazed brightly on both sides of the staircase, illuminating the night.

"What perfect timing! I'm on my way to Paris, to the Palais-Royal! Join me!" she said, waving Belle over.

"Paris?" Belle echoed. "But how? This isn't *real* . . . it's only a story."

"One that *I'm* writing, as I told you before," the countess said, pointing her fan at Belle. "Would you like your story to include Paris?"

Belle nodded. It was too much to hope for.

The countess smiled. "Then it *will*. Now climb in, my sweet child. My horses are impatient creatures."

The Palais-Royal! Belle thought, her heart dancing. She'd heard of it. Who hadn't? It was the most exciting place in all of Paris. Everyone who was anyone strolled its courts or sat in its cafés—writers and philosophers, professors and princesses, circus girls and opera singers.

Belle had stepped through *Nevermore* and into the grounds of the countess's estate only moments ago. Moonlight had illuminated the gravel drive, and as Belle had hurried up it, she'd seen that the roses dotting the estate had grown bushier in her absence, and the yew trees taller. In some places, the yews had grown together so thickly that they made solid hedges.

Mouchard opened the carriage door now. Belle skirted around one of the stone lions at the bottom of the steps, and Mouchard helped her up. After the two women shared a quick embrace, Belle sat down across from the countess, fluffing her skirts around her.

Once again, she found herself dressed perfectly for the

occasion, this time in a sky-blue gown sprigged with white flowers. A length of delicate white lace was knotted around her shoulders. Her hair was gathered in a loose, cascading ponytail.

The countess herself was dressed in a gown of black sateen with an embroidered black silk wrap. Several strands of flawless black pearls circled her throat.

She's always in black. She must be a widow, Belle thought.

"Off we go," the countess said, rapping on the side of the carriage with her silver-topped walking stick.

Mouchard hopped up next to the driver, and the carriage rolled down the drive and out of the gates. The countess's estate was just outside Paris, and it wasn't long before they were in the city's bustling heart.

Flickering streetlamps cast their glow over elegant mansions, stately townhouses, and manicured squares. Well-dressed people strolled the streets. Restaurants and cafés were lit up. Music spilled out of their doors.

Even though it was late, Paris was noisy, alive, and captivating—so much so that Belle's frustration with the Beast, her loneliness, and her sadness, were soon forgotten.

"Paris," the countess said dreamily. "There's nothing like it, is there?"

"It's breathtaking," said Belle. "Thank you so much for bringing me here. You're too good to me."

Why? Belle wondered. *Why is she so good to me?*

She was about to ask, but before she could, the countess spoke.

"It makes me happy to make you happy, Belle," she said. "I'm sure the Palais will be highly entertaining tonight. I'm told there's a fire-eater newly arrived from Delhi. And a sword-swallower from Budapest. You'll love them. Tell me, have you ever been there?"

Belle shook her head. "No, I—" she started to say. But the countess barely let her get a word in.

"No?!" she exclaimed, clutching her pearls. "My child, we must get you out more. You're in for a treat. It used to be a king's palace. Now it's a pleasure garden, with theaters, shops, and cafes. Actors, acrobats, musicians—they all perform in the center courtyard. It's spectacular! Ah, here we are now!"

Mouchard jumped down and was on the sidewalk as the carriage stopped, ready to hand the women down. The Palais, all pillars, pediments, and airy galleries, took Belle's breath away. The countess led her through an arched entryway down a long colonnade. Belle was captivated by the beautiful boutiques that greeted them, selling everything from shoes studded with pearls, to cakes topped with gold leaf, to books sporting jeweled covers.

As they strolled, the countess leaned in close to Belle.

"Do you see that woman over there?" she whispered, nodding at a lady in a crimson dress. "She's from Vienna. Rumor has it she spies for the Austrian queen and keeps a pistol in her garter."

Belle's eyes shone with excitement. "Do you think we can meet her?" she asked.

"I shall arrange it," the countess replied. She nodded at an elderly woman with a black eye patch and a monkey on her shoulder. "She's one of the wealthiest women in France. Made her fortune smuggling rum."

The countess led Belle to a stylish café. They were seated outside, near a row of flowering crabapple trees in giant terracotta pots. Candles flickered on every table.

A waiter arrived immediately, bearing porcelain cups as thin as eggshells. He poured coffee into them, then set a plate of sweets on the table. Among them were small pink tea cakes with candied rose petals on top. Marzipan hearts with sugared violets. Candied chestnuts. Cream puffs. Tiny custard tarts. Belle thought them almost too pretty to eat.

"How divine!" the countess said, her fingers hovering over

the plate. "Belle, you must eat every one—to keep me from doing so."

Belle chose a tea cake. As she popped it into her mouth, the countess said, "Is that all? You'll waste away. Do have some more."

The countess herself selected a tiny mille-feuille. Its brittle layers shattered as she bit into it. Licking pastry shards from her red lips, she said, "That man, there?" Her eyes darted to an elegant gentleman wearing several large jeweled rings. "He's an Italian count. A Borgia, my dear. Diabolically charming, but never, *ever* accept an invitation to dinner. And the woman next to him, the one wearing *far* too much rouge . . ."

As the countess continued to gossip, Belle listened raptly, fascinated by the exotic people all around her and the lives of intrigue and mystery they lived. The balmy night, the graceful Palais, the elegant café—they were all so lovely.

So far, Paris was everything that tiny, provincial Villeneuve was not, and Belle adored it.

"I'm having such fun chatting with you, Belle. Truly," the countess said. "I hope you're enjoying yourself, too."

"Enjoying myself?" said Belle, laughing. "Madame Comtesse, this is exactly what I needed."

The countess leaned back in her chair and looked up at

the night sky, smiling at the twinkling stars. "Your parents lived very near here when they were young. Did you know that?" she asked. "In a tiny garret apartment. I met them years ago. I met you, too."

"You did? When?" asked Belle. Surely, she would recall meeting someone as grand and glamorous as the countess, but she couldn't.

"It was a *long* time ago," the countess said, training her gaze on Belle again. "You were only a baby in your mother's arms."

Belle looked at the countess wonderingly. "You were friends, you and my mother?" she asked.

The countess smiled. "Indeed. I am a great admirer of your father's work, you see. And I've acquired many of his music boxes over the years." The countess's smile turned wistful. "I was with her at the very end, you know. Mine was the last face she ever saw."

"But my father . . . I thought he . . ." Belle started to say.

"Oh, he was there, too. Of course he was," the countess assured Belle. "We both were."

"He doesn't like to talk about her," Belle said, dropping her gaze. She smiled sadly. "It's always been too painful for him."

"You miss him very much, don't you?"

CHAPTER TWENTY-TWO

"I do," Belle said. "He was my world and I was his."

"Your mother felt the same way," the countess said. "She loved him very much."

"What was she like, my mother?" Belle asked, hungry to learn about the woman she'd never known.

"Kind. Smart. Beautiful. Just like you," the countess said. "I liked her very much. And I know she would be distraught if she'd lived to see what's happened to you." She paused for a few seconds, her eyes seeking Belle's, then said, "Which is why I did it."

Belle cocked her head, puzzled. "Why you did what, my lady?"

"Why I sent you *Nevermore.*"

CHAPTER TWENTY-THREE

"*YOU SENT NEVERMORE?*" Belle said, astonished. "I thought it was one of the Beast's books."

"I had a servant steal into the Beast's castle and place the book there. I hoped you would find it. I want to help you, Belle. I want to widen the scope of your story."

"How?"

"By giving you a way out of your prison. By allowing you to see something of the world and its people. To visit the great cities and study at the great universities. Anything is possible here in *Nevermore*."

Belle stared at the countess, speechless. What she was offering . . . it was nothing less than a dream come true. To see not only Paris, but Padua and Prague and dozens other such places? To study at places like the Sorbonne or Oxford? These were opportunities Belle had longed for, but never, ever expected to have.

As excited as she was, the same question she'd had when they'd first arrived at the Palais-Royal pushed at her again now. The countess was so kind to her, so generous. It was almost too much.

"Why?" Belle asked. "Madame Comtesse, why are you doing so much for me?"

The countess reached across the table and took Belle's hands in hers. "In honor of your dear mother's memory, Belle. Because I know that making you happy would make her happy. Would you like that? To see a bit of the world? Will you come traveling with me?"

Belle flew from her chair and hugged the countess. "Nothing could stop me. Thank you, my lady. *Thank you.*"

"You're very welcome, child," said the countess, patting Belle's back. "But your happiness is all the thanks I need."

"How will you do it?" Belle asked, sitting down again. "How will you get us to all of these places?"

The countess wagged a finger at Belle. "You must let the author keep her secrets, child."

As she was speaking, the hulking Mouchard appeared. He

bent low to the countess and whispered something in her ear. Her smile slipped. Her eyes darkened.

"*What?* But she has no business here!" she said. "Are you certain you saw her? Where?"

Mouchard nodded at the café.

"Is everything all right?" Belle asked, concerned.

"It appears that a relative of mine is inside the café," the countess explained, with a tight smile. "I must go and say hello. Will you excuse me for a moment?"

"Of course," said Belle.

"I won't be long," the countess said, rising. "Finish the sweets, Belle. And think about our first destination!"

Belle nodded eagerly. She was so happy, she was almost giddy. It was all she could do not to jump out of her seat and dance around the café. Trying to calm herself, she reached for the plate of pastries.

As she did, a large brown spider dropped out of the tree branches above and landed smack in the middle of it.

CHAPTER TWENTY-FOUR

LOVE WATCHED AS DEATH APPROACHED HER.

"Good evening, *comtesse*," she said, sarcasm dripping from her voice.

She was seated at a table for two. Her silvery hair was piled high on her head. Ropes of white pearls hung from her neck. She wore a fitted jacket of white silk and a voluminous matching skirt.

Death sat down across from her. "This is *my* realm, and I don't recall extending you an invitation," she said. "Why are you here?"

"Because you're cheating, dear sister. *Again.* And you need to stop."

Death affected a look of innocence. "Whatever gave you that idea?"

Love ignored the question. "Nothing left up your sleeve, is there? You've played all your cards. A lavish ball. A handsome duke. The promise of travel, of an education. Why, you've even played the mother card. Have you *no* shame?"

"All I'm doing is providing a harmless escape for the poor girl," Death said airily. "Which is more than *you* can say. What a bore her life must be, shut up in that dreary castle day after day, with that awful Beast and all his talking bric-a-brac."

"That is a *lie*. I know exactly what you're up to."

Death gave her sister a smug smile. "Do you?"

"As powerful as you are, you can't take a life before its time," Love said, "so you're trying to bind Belle to *Nevermore*."

Death held out her hand and inspected her sharp red nails. "I haven't the *faintest* idea what you're talking about."

"You're playing by the Rule of Three," said Love. "Named for the three Fates, the first of whom holds the spool upon which the thread of life is wound; the second, who pulls that thread; and the third, who snips it. If Belle eats three things in *Nevermore*, and leave three things, she'll be bound to it."

Death lowered her hand. She met her sister's gaze. "This is becoming tedious. If I admit to it, will you leave?" she asked.

"I *knew* it," Love said, shaking her head.

"Can you blame me? It's such an elegant rule, don't you agree?" Death said. "Beginning, middle, and ending—all lives have them, and so do all stories. Though I must admit, I'm partial to the ending."

"Well, you won't get one," said Love briskly. "Belle hasn't left anything in *Nevermore*."

"Are you certain?" Death purred.

"Quite," said Love. "She didn't eat much at your ball, either. Despite your best efforts. My beetles saw to that."

"She did just now, though," said Death.

Love's green eyes flashed with anger. "She won't do it again. Not if I can help it!"

Death shot forward in her chair. "But you *can't*, Sister dear. This is *my* story. You don't belong here. Leave. *Now.* Or I shall call my servant to throw you out."

Love glanced at Death's henchman. He was lurking near the door. A shudder ran through her. "How do you stand having that horrible creature around?" she asked. "He stinks of the grave."

"That happens to be my favorite perfume," Death said. "Mouchard! Come!"

But Love was too quick for him. With a flourish of white silk, she'd crossed the café, slipped through the kitchen door, and disappeared.

"Shall I follow her, madame?" Mouchard asked.

"Yes, make sure she's *really* gone," Death said. "And keep her out from now on. Get the others to help you."

Mouchard dipped his head. "Very good, madame," he said, starting for the door to the kitchen, his black eyes bright and beady.

Death remained where she was for a moment, drumming her fingers on the table. It was worrisome that Love had discovered what she was up to. She would never heed the warning to stay away; on the contrary, she would try twice as hard to meddle. Mouchard and a dozen more vultures would make it hard for her, though.

Nonetheless, Death knew she had to step up her efforts. And she would.

"My sister is wrong. As usual," she whispered. "I still have one card up my sleeve. The best card of all."

She gazed out of the window as she spoke. She couldn't see Belle, but she knew she was there, sitting at her table, happily watching the world go by.

"And I intend to play it."

CHAPTER TWENTY-FIVE

BELLE GASPED. She pushed her chair back from the table. She wasn't particularly afraid of large brown spiders, but she also wasn't accustomed to them standing in her food.

As she watched, the spider crawled over the pastries, her long, spiky legs sinking into the icing. As she reached the edge of the platter, a glossy black beetle landed on the table. Belle realized that it was the same beetle that had appeared at the countess's ball. She recognized his shimmering wings.

A few of the café's patrons noticed him and made faces, but kept right on eating. Belle glanced around for the countess, but she was still inside the café.

"Would you . . . would you like a sweet?" she asked the beetle, picking one up off the platter and offering it to him.

The beetle reared up on his hind legs and angrily smacked the pastry away with his fearsome horns.

"You're being fed *lies*, foolish girl!" he said, pointing a claw at her.

Belle's eyebrows shot up. "You can *speak*?" she asked, amazed.

"Clearly," he replied. "Stop eating things. It's dangerous in *Nevermore*."

"Don't be silly. How can little pink cakes be dangerous?" Belle asked.

Her tone was scornful, but as the words were leaving her mouth, a chilly sense of uneasiness stole over her. This was the second time the beetle had tried to warn her away from food.

The beetle didn't answer. He looked around anxiously, picked up a custard tart, and threw it on the ground. The spider did the same with a cream puff.

"Stop that!" Belle scolded, angered. "That's rude, beetle!"

"Lucanos," said the beetle haughtily, shoving a candied chestnut off the table. "My name is Lucanos, not *beetle*. My friend here is Aranae."

"Why mustn't I eat any food? Who sent you?" Belle

demanded. She remembered that the countess had told her that a madwoman owned the bugs, and that sometime they escaped. Had they flown all the way from the countryside to Paris? Or had the madwoman brought them here herself? Was she nearby? Belle looked over her shoulder nervously.

"The *who* part is not important," the beetle said. "What *is* important is that you understand the Rule of Three. If you eat things, or leave things—" He abruptly stopped speaking. His eyes darted to the right.

Belle followed his gaze, expecting to see a crazed person bearing down on her. Instead she saw the countess returning.

"Hurry, Aranae!" Lucanos said.

Working together, the beetle and the spider quickly pushed the entire plate of sweets off the table. It shattered loudly. Lucanos flew away. Aranae scuttled off.

"My word!" the countess exclaimed. "What happened?"

Belle told her.

"Disgusting creatures! But at least they're gone now. The madwoman didn't approach you, did she?" she asked.

"No," Belle said.

"Good. That's a relief. She's capable of anything, Belle. You don't ever want to find yourself alone with her," said the countess gravely.

Belle nodded. "Did you find your relative?" she asked.

The countess smiled. "I did. We had a lovely chat. I would have introduced you, but she was in a bit of a hurry."

She motioned a waiter over and paid their bill. "I must return home now," she said. "It's getting late, and I should get some rest. You should, too, Belle. After all, we have much planning to do! Rome is lovely this time of year. Or maybe Florence?"

The countess kept talking, and Belle, carried away by her descriptions of Italy, was only too happy to listen. Her uneasiness about Lucanos and his strange warnings, and her bafflement over how they would get to places like Rome and Florence, evaporated as the countess rhapsodized over the ceiling of the Sistine Chapel or the shops along the Ponte Vecchio.

Arm in arm, they strolled back toward the carriage. On the way, they stopped in the Palais's courtyard, where they watched a troupe of acrobats from Shanghai, conjurers from Zanzibar, and a magician from Constantinople.

"Oh, look!" the countess suddenly said, pointing to the center of the yard. "Monsieur Truqué is here. His creations are the best in Paris, Belle. You simply *must* see them!"

She tugged on Belle's arm, hurrying her to a striped marquee. Torches blazed at either side of it. Under it were three people. Each was perfectly still. The first, a gentleman, was seated at a harpsichord, his head bent. Another, a king with a crown on his head, was frozen in a bow. Across from him, a queen was executing a curtsy.

Only as Belle drew closer did she realize that they were automatons. Their heads and hands were papier-mâché; their gracious smiles were painted on; their eyes were glass.

Other spectators joined Belle and the countess. *"That's Truqué himself!"* one whispered, pointing to the right of the marquee. A wiry bald man stood there, one hand folded over the other. Ruffles from his white shirt spilled out from his long gray coat. His eyes were sharp and watchful.

After a moment, he gave a shrill, squawking cough, and a hush fell over the crowed. When they were perfectly quiet, he pulled a large brass key from the pocket of his coat.

"The key to life!" he intoned, holding it high.

Then he walked over to the harpsichord player, inserted the key in his back, and turned it. An awestruck "Oh!" rose from the crowd as the player's hands moved over the keys and the notes of a minuet were heard.

Monsieur Truqué then wound the queen. Her chest expanded just as if she were really drawing a breath. She rose from her curtsy, lifted her head, and smiled.

It was the king's turn next. He straightened slowly and

offered the queen his hand. The two began to dance, their movements jerky and shuddering at first, then graceful.

"I give you King Otto and Queen Matilda!" Monsieur Truqué shouted.

The audience applauded.

"They are remarkable, are they not?" the countess whispered to Belle.

For a few magical moments, Belle almost believed the figures were human. But then they began to slow. The musician's sleeve slid back slightly as he played, revealing the metal joints of his wrists. His head drooped. His hands froze. The music stopped. The queen's legs stiffened. Her smile hardened.

The king, who'd been the last to be wound, danced alone for a few seconds, and then he, too, began to slow. The cogs and gears that animated him juddered to a halt. His legs stopped. His shoulders sagged. In the instant before his eyes closed, they met Belle's. The look in them was so full of longing, the Belle's heart hurt for him. He thrust a hand out, reaching for her, then slumped over, his head hanging.

"Oh!" Belle cried. "Poor King Otto!"

The countess turned to her. "What's the matter, child?" she asked.

"He looked so sad, my lady. As if he wanted so much to be alive."

CHAPTER TWENTY-FIVE

"He did, yes," the countess said thoughtfully.

A small boy moved among the crowd, cap in hand, collecting money for Truqué. Seeing him, the countess reached into a small silk purse she was carrying and drew out a silver coin.

Belle had been so moved by the performance that she wanted to contribute, too.

The night she'd left Villeneuve in search of her father, she'd quickly grabbed a few sous as she'd run out of her house in case she needed any money. The small copper coins were not worth much, but they were all she'd had. She'd kept them in the pocket of her blue work dress, together with her linen handkerchief, as small, touchable reminders of home. *Nevermore* had transformed that dress into a beautiful gown. Would the coins still be in the pocket?

She searched the skirts of the gown to see if they contained any pockets. Finding one, she dipped her hand inside it. Her fingers closed on her small copper coins. Her handkerchief was there, too.

Drawing two coins out, she waited for the boy to approach.

"That's so kind of you, Belle," the countess said approvingly.

"I only wish it was more," said Belle.

"Nonsense. Whatever you give will be much appreciated.

Here's the young fellow now. Go ahead . . ." the countess urged.

The boy came up to them, smiling. The countess dropped her coin in his cap. Belle was just about to do the same when, out of nowhere, a woman thrust herself between Belle and the little boy. She pushed Belle away, snatched the cap out of the child's hands, and ran off with it.

It happened so fast, Belle didn't have time even to gasp. The woman was wearing a hat with a veil. Belle saw nothing of her face. All she caught was a swirl of white skirts, and then the woman was gone.

"Stop, thief!" Truqué yelled.

"Catch her!" bellowed a man in the crowd.

"Hurry, she's getting away!" shouted a woman.

But it was too late. The woman was already on the far side of the courtyard. She ducked through a doorway and disappeared.

"Did she . . . did she just *steal* the little boy's cap?" Belle asked, outraged. Her hands were shaking. She put her coins back in her pocket, certain she would drop them if she didn't.

"I believe she did," the countess said. She was still staring after the thief. Her eyes were smoldering with anger.

"Where did she come from?" Belle asked.

"She was lurking in the shadows, most likely, waiting for her chance," the countess said.

That made no sense to Belle. Wasn't *Nevermore* the countess's book?

"But Madame Comtesse, you are writing this story," Belle said. "How can such a person push her way into it if you don't wish it?"

"Ah, Belle. That is every writer's lament," the countess replied, sighing. "These troublesome characters! They do as they wish, and we authors have little to say about it." Taking Belle's arm again, she added, "Poor child! You're trembling. Come, we *must* find Mouchard and the carriage. I believe we've had enough excitement for one night."

She led Belle away from Truqué, his marquee, and the milling crowd.

Distracted by a man at the edge of the courtyard, who was juggling a hatchet, a small dog, and a pineapple, Belle didn't notice as the countess's gaze slid back to Monsieur Truqué.

She didn't see Truqué nod at the countess.

And pat the lifeless king.

And smile.

CHAPTER TWENTY-SIX

CLOUDS MOVED IN ACROSS THE SKY, obscuring the moon and stars.

The night air was cool and felt as soft as velvet on Belle's face as the carriage ferried her and the countess out of the city and back to the countryside.

As the excitement of the evening ebbed away, Belle's eyes became heavy. By the time they arrived back at the château, she was hiding yawns behind her hand.

Mouchard was down out of his seat, his hand on the door, before the carriage had even stopped.

"Goodbye, Madame Comtesse," Belle said as they stepped into the drive. "And thank you again for everything."

There was a note of melancholy in Belle's voice. The countess noticed it. "What's the matter, child?" she asked.

"Nothing," Belle said wistfully. "At least, nothing that doesn't make me sound like a complete ingrate. I just . . . I wish I didn't have to leave. Ever. I wish *Nevermore* was real."

The countess smoothed a stray piece of hair off Belle's forehead. Her touch was as cool as marble. "Does it matter if it's not?" she asked. "Life can be so difficult, and stories help us escape those difficulties. It's all right to lose yourself in one, Belle. Isn't that what you've *always* done? And this one is your own story, for goodness' sake! What harm can there possibly be in *that*?"

Belle nodded. The countess was right.

"You're very tired, my child, that's all," the countess said. "Get some sleep, and then come back to me just as soon as you can."

She kissed Belle's forehead, her lips icy against Belle's skin, and then she was gone in a cloud of black, up the stone steps and into her mansion. The doors boomed shut after her.

Mouchard cleared his throat. "This way, mademoiselle, if you please," he said in a voice as dolorous as a tolling bell.

Belle followed him across the large, graveled circle in front of the château, in which carriages turned around, to the drive's narrow mouth. To her amazement, the leafy green trees had grown shaggier, the yew trees closer together, the rosebushes thornier, during the few hours she and the countess had been at the Palais-Royal.

"The way back . . . is it still down there?" she asked.

"It's right where it always has been, mademoiselle," Mouchard replied, handing her the candle she'd been carrying when she'd entered *Nevermore*.

Belle blinked into the gloom. "I don't suppose you have a lamp I could borrow. Something a bit brighter than this candle?" she asked, glancing back at Mouchard.

But he was gone.

The sense of unease Belle had felt earlier returned as she started walking. The rose canes reached for Belle like long, greedy fingers. Thorns snagged her skirt. She pulled it free and kept going.

As she walked under a canopy of towering oaks, the darkness deepened. The rustling of night creatures filled her ears. An owl called; its plaintive *whoo* sent shivers up Belle's spine. Tree roots snaked over the ground, threatening to trip her.

A fat brown toad as big as a cat hopped onto the path in front of her, making her jump. Its golden eyes followed her as she gingerly stepped around it.

The farther she walked down the drive, the more it

narrowed and twisted. A cold dread pooled in her chest. "What if I can't find my way back to the book?" she whispered.

At that moment, a figure appeared in front of her. He stood as tall as a man and wore a man's clothing, but he had a long snout, pointed ears, and pointed teeth, too. Just like a wolf.

Belle's heart started to hammer.

"W-who are you?" she stammered. "What do you want?"

The man didn't answer her.

The moon came out from behind the cloud just then. Belle saw that it wasn't a real person at all, only a hedge cut to resemble one.

Belle walked on. She took another turn, and one more, and then there it was, right in front of her—the giant book with its shimmering pages. But the shimmering silver seemed denser now, and pushing her hand through it was like pushing it into a bowl of porridge. She stepped through with effort and found herself back in the Beast's library.

She was in her nightclothes again. Her candle was still in her hand. Her heartbeat had returned to something like normal, but she still felt fearful.

Why was it so much harder to get back to the Beast's castle this time? she wondered.

The dense hedges, the twining roots and branches that had seemed to clutch at her . . . it almost felt as if *Nevermore* wanted to keep her there.

Lucanos had told her that she was being fed lies. Was he right? Should she be wary of *Nevermore*?

Belle shook her head, convinced that she was merely letting her tiredness get the better of her.

Surely the comtesse would have told me if I had anything to fear from the story, she reasoned. *And why should I listen to that beetle anyway? He's probably every bit as insane as his owner.*

The countess was right. Life could be difficult. Lonely, too. Confusing at times. Frustrating. Often sad.

But *Nevermore* was none of those things. It was beautiful and fascinating. Inspiring. Surprising. Glamorous and fun.

The countess's voice echoed in her memory . . . *come back to me just as soon as you can.*

"I will, Madame Comtesse," Belle whispered to the darkness. "Just as soon as I can."

CHAPTER TWENTY-SEVEN

"I *KNEW* SKATING WAS a terrible idea," Cogsworth said. "What if it's *not* a cold? What if it's bronchitis? Or pneumonia?" He lowered his voice. "What if it's the black plague?"

Lumiere, who was checking the Beast's breakfast tray, gave him a look. "The black plague," he said flatly. "Which hasn't been seen in these parts for a hundred years . . . *that* black plague?"

"It's a cold, Mr. Cogsworth, that's all," said Mrs. Potts, bustling by. "The master caught a chill whilst skating. With rest and good care, he'll soon be right as rain."

Belle was seated at the large kitchen table with Chip. She

was eating her breakfast: brioche with jam, a bowl of oatmeal with raisins and cream, and milky hot chocolate.

Belle was exhausted. By the time she'd hidden *Nevermore* away again and let herself out of the library, dawn had been breaking—too late to catch up on her lost sleep. She'd hurried back to her bedroom, where she'd washed her face, brushed her hair, and dressed. Then she'd joined Mrs. Potts, Chip, and the others in the kitchen.

Chapeau picked up the Beast's tray now and headed out of the kitchen. Lumiere and Cogsworth followed him, their conversation trailing them.

"A good hot footbath would be just the thing to fend off a bout of malaria," Cogsworth said.

"It's malaria now, Dr. Cogsworth?" said Lumiere. "Your ridiculous imagination is the only thing that we really have to fear."

"I only *hope* it's malaria," said Cogsworth darkly. "It could be leprosy."

Plumette was already hard at work dusting the music room. Maestro Cadenza, the castle's harpsichord, had been complaining that an excess of dust was making his keys stick. Froufrou was patrolling for rats. Madame de Garderobe, a tall gilt dresser in Belle's bedroom, was mending a pinafore that Belle had torn.

As usual, the servants all had chores to do, Chip had his studies to attend to, and now the Beast was laid up in bed. Another long, lonely day stretched out in front of Belle, full of nothing to do and no one to do it with. She couldn't wait to get back to *Nevermore*.

She finished her breakfast, cleared up her dishes, and was about to head to the library when Mrs. Potts asked her if she would take a bowl of stale bread crumbs to the chickens. Chip volunteered to go with her. Chapeau had gone upstairs, so Belle hurried out of the kitchen to the coatroom to find her cloak and mittens.

Mrs. Potts quietly followed her out and met her in the hallway as she was returning. "Belle, do you have a minute?" she asked. Her voice was low. She glanced behind herself as she spoke.

"Of course, Mrs. Potts. Is there something wrong?" Belle asked.

"No, I just don't want Chip to hear me. His birthday is tomorrow. I'm planning a little surprise party for him tomorrow night, and I was wondering if I could ask you to make some decorations."

"I'd love to!" Belle said, happy to help. It would delay her return to *Nevermore*, but only by an hour or so, and there was nothing she wouldn't do for Chip.

"Thank you, Belle," said Mrs. Potts, pleased. "Cuisinier's baking a cake, and I have a little present for him, too."

Belle and Mrs. Potts started back to the kitchen, planning the best way to carry out the surprise. As Belle reached out to push the kitchen door open, Mrs. Potts stopped her.

Frowning, she said, "You look so pale this morning, child. There are shadows as deep as midnight under your eyes, and I saw you yawning constantly during breakfast. You're not coming down with a cold, too, are you?"

"I'm fine," Belle said, forcing a smile. "Just a little tired. I couldn't sleep last night, so I got up to make some hot milk."

"And went back to bed?"

"And went to the library," Belle admitted sheepishly.

Mrs. Potts's frown deepened. "You only just found out about the library, and already you're spending so much time there, Belle. So much time alone."

"I only intended to read for a little while," she quickly explained, "but I . . . um, I got lost in a good book."

Belle felt a twinge of guilt at not being completely honest, but she felt that Mrs. Potts would worry even more if she knew about *Nevermore*, and about Belle's plans to spend as much time as possible there.

"Belle . . ." said Mrs. Potts, giving her a searching glance.

"Yes, Mrs. Potts?"

"I know it's very hard . . . your situation here. With the master. With all of us. I know this isn't your choice. . . ." She hesitated, trying to find the right words, then said, "Belle, it's a wonderful thing to read about other people's lives, but it's important to live your own life, too—no matter how challenging that life may sometimes be. Do you understand what I'm telling you, child?"

Before Belle could answer, the kitchen door burst open.

"Belle!" Chip shouted at the top of his lungs.

"My goodness, Chip! Could you possibly be any louder?" Mrs. Potts scolded.

"Sorry, Mama," Chip said. He turned to Belle. "Come on, Belle, let's go!"

"I understand, Mrs. Potts. And I'm fine, really," Belle said. And then she hurried after Chip, relieved that the conversation was over. She was spending a lot of time in the library, yes—but not by herself.

Belle grabbed the bowl of crumbs, and then she and Chip banged out of the back door and headed for the chicken coop.

She never saw Mrs. Potts at the window, watching them go, a sigh rattling her lid and worry etching another tiny crack in her painted porcelain face.

CHAPTER TWENTY-EIGHT

"MAMA SAYS THE MASTER feels awful," Chip said, chattering away. "She says he's got a terrible cough and sniffles. And that he's very cranky."

"The Beast, cranky? I don't believe it," Belle joked.

Chip laughed. "I was going to visit him with Froufrou to try to cheer him up, but Mama said no. She said we'll give him a relaugh. What's wrong with that, Belle? Lumiere says laughter is the best medicine."

"I think she meant *relapse*, Chip."

"Oh," Chip said, his little face falling. "Well, there must be *something* we can do."

Just then, Belle stumbled and spilled some of the crumbs. A tiny sparrow immediately swooped down to peck at them.

Which gave her an idea.

"Come on, Chip!" she said excitedly, veering off toward the West Wing.

"But what about the chickens?" Chip asked.

"We'll bring them some cracked wheat later," she called over her shoulder.

When they reached the snow-covered west lawn, Belle took her mittens off and started sprinkling the crumbs on the ground, making careful, deliberate lines.

"What are we doing, Belle?" Chip asked, watching her.

"We're writing a message for him," she replied.

"But, Belle, it won't work. The master won't see the crumbs. They won't show up against the snow."

"He'll see them. I promise!" Belle said.

Chip looked unconvinced, but he followed her as she worked. When she was finished, she put her mittens back on and walked toward the Beast's window. A lark trilled loudly from a tree. It flapped its wings and flew down to the crumbs.

"See, Belle? The birds are going to eat up all the crumbs!" Chip cried.

"That's the whole idea!" said Belle, grinning. "Now we've just got to get his attention!"

She bent down, scooped up some snow, and patted it together. She launched her snowball at the Beast's window and hit it dead center. But nothing happened. No one appeared at the panes.

"Try again!" Chip urged.

Belle scraped up more snow, packed it tightly, and then wound up. An instant after she fired the snowball, the window suddenly opened. Cogsworth stuck his head out . . . and took a speeding missile straight to the face.

"Oh, no!" Belle cried, her hands coming up to her mouth.

Chip quickly hid behind her skirts.

"Raise the drawbridge! Lower the portcullis!" Cogsworth bellowed, wiping the snow away. "We're under attack!"

Lumiere came to the window. He pulled Cogsworth away and peered out.

"Lumiere!" Belle called out. "Over here!"

Lumiere spotted her. He smiled and waved.

"Tell Cogsworth I'm sorry!" Belle shouted.

"Do I have to?" Lumiere shouted back.

"*Yes!* And can you get the Beast?"

Lumiere nodded, then disappeared into the room.

A few seconds later, the Beast appeared in his dressing

gown, scowling—but the moment he saw Belle, in her blue cloak with her cheeks rosy from the cold, waving like mad, he smiled.

"Look at the lawn!" she shouted.

The Beast tilted his head; he held a paw to his ear.

"He can't hear us!" said Chip.

Belle cupped her hands to her mouth. "LOOK OVER THERE!" she yelled, then pointed to where she had placed the crumbs.

The Beast turned his head. His smile broadened into laughter.

Dozens of birds—sparrows, cuckoos, magpies, ouzels, and larks—had spotted the tasty crumbs. They'd flown out of the woods and landed in the snow, eager to peck them up. Their quick, busy bodies formed living letters, spelling out a message: GET WELL SOON!

"The master loves it, Belle!" Chip crowed. "I've never seen him laugh so much!"

The sound of the Beast's laughter gladdened Belle. As she watched him, she was pierced by the realization that she missed him. The castle wasn't the same with him shut up in his room.

Why? she asked herself. *How could I miss this quick-tempered, touchy, cantankerous creature?*

Because he's also funny, caring, and kind, a voice inside her replied.

Unfortunately, the Beast's laughter soon turned into a deep, hacking cough, and Cogsworth appeared in the window again, glaring at Belle and Chip.

The Beast made an *oh, no!* face and pretended to bite his claws.

Belle and Chip giggled. Cogsworth did not. He ushered the Beast away from the window and slammed it shut, but not before the Beast gave Belle and Chip one last wave.

"Well, Chip, if laughter really is the best medicine, then I'd say we've cured him," Belle declared.

The two made their way to the feed room of the castle's stone barn and scooped some cracked wheat from a sack. They fed the chickens, then returned to the kitchen. As soon as Mrs. Potts saw Chip, she told him that she expected him to spend a good hour studying his multiplication tables.

Chip groaned, but he settled himself at the kitchen table with a magic slate and piece of chalk that wrote out the tables as he dictated them.

Belle gave him a sympathetic smile, then left so she wouldn't distract him. Out in the hallway, Chapeau took her cloak. She headed upstairs, planning to make her bed, tidy her room, and then find something—paper, maybe some fabric scraps—out of which she could fashion decorations for Chip's party.

She was alone again. There was no one to sit with. No one to talk to. But she comforted herself with the knowledge that she would be with the countess again shortly. They would make their travel plans today. Her heart leapt at the thought.

Where would they go first? London? Madrid? Berlin? Athens?

Belle had spent her life in a tiny provincial village, and now, almost overnight, the world, with all its people and cultures, its castles and ruins, its universities and museums, was at her fingertips.

Nevermore was more than the countess.

It was more than a book, more than a story.

It was like nothing she'd ever known.

And everything she'd ever wanted.

CHAPTER TWENTY-NINE

BELLE LOWERED THE WINDOW in the countess's carriage and leaned out. The wind would muss her hair. The sun would freckle her nose. But she didn't care.

Her excitement grew as the carriage turned off the narrow lane and rolled up a hill toward a set of gates. She'd escaped into *Nevermore* half an hour ago and found herself dressed for a garden party in a blue-and-yellow day dress and a straw hat with ribbons.

Mouchard had met her in the courtyard.

"Her Ladyship is in the summer house this morning, at the west end of the estate," he informed her. "She asks that you join her there. I have readied a coach. Enclosed this time, mademoiselle, to protect you from the sun."

The carriage was light and quick. It flew over the dirt roads that wound through the deep woods of the countess's grounds.

She must own thousands of acres, Belle thought, for the ride lasted a good thirty minutes. She reminded herself to keep track of the passing time. Chip's party was that evening. She must allow herself time enough to get back to the Beast's castle and help get things ready.

Finally, woods and meadows gave way to manicured lawns and a drive lined by chestnut trees in full flower. The drive snaked past ponds framed by willows and graced by swans. A warm breeze blew as the carriage rolled through rose gardens. It tugged petals from the blooms and swirled them through the air like colorful confetti. Belle laughed out loud, delighted by the spectacle.

Just as she was thinking that she had never, ever seen any place as beautiful as this, the summer house itself came into view. Goggle-eyed, she sat up straight, whacking her head on the window frame.

The coach entered a courtyard flanked by formal lawns and flowering trees. At the end of it, a curved stairway led to the entry of a two-story dwelling, built of yellow limestone and bookended by two round towers.

"A *summer house?*" Belle whispered in disbelief. "This is a miniature palace!"

The carriage slowed as it approached the stairs. Belle quickly patted her hair into place and put her hat on, tying the ribbons under her chin. The ever-present Mouchard jumped down from his seat next to the driver to help her out.

As Belle alighted, a movement caught her eye. The countess, wearing her customary black, was descending the stone steps, skirts sweeping over them. Her dark hair was pinned up loosely. Ropes of jet-black beads hung from her neck. Four elegant greyhounds followed her.

"My darling girl!" she cried as she embraced Belle. "I'm so glad to see you!"

"Nothing could have kept me away, my lady," said Belle.

"Come inside," the countess urged, grabbing Belle's hand. "There's someone I'd like you to meet. A special friend of mine, just arrived from Italy."

The two women hurried up the steps. Belle soon saw that just as with the countess's château, the summer house was filled with beautiful men and women sipping tea in sumptuously decorated rooms, strolling through the gardens, or fanning themselves on the terraces.

But the countess had no time to introduce Belle to any of them. Instead, she rushed her straight into her study.

The room was lined with floor-to-ceiling bookcases on all four walls. Belle was delighted to see that many of the shelves contained music boxes made by her father. Forgetting that she was supposed to be meeting the countess's friend, she walked to the shelves and touched one.

It was a small one, modeled after a cottage. Belle had never seen the music box before. He must've made it before she was born. She pictured him leaning over his workbench, placing each of the mill's shingles so carefully, and tears threatened. As they always did when she was missing her father.

"Belle?"

It was the countess. Remembering where she was, Belle blinked her tears away and turned around, a smile on her face.

"Belle, may I present Professore Armando Truffatore?" the countess said. "Professore, this is my dear friend Mademoiselle Belle."

Belle dipped a neat curtsy to the professor. As she rose, he took her hand and kissed it.

"The professor is from the Università di Bologna, one of Italy's oldest universities," the countess explained. "He teaches the classics there, and I thought he would be the *perfect* person to help us devise our travel itinerary." She paused, then said, "That is, if you still wish to go abroad."

"Yes, of course!" Belle said, trying to put the music boxes out of her mind.

"Come, signorina," the professor said with a charming Italian accent, gesturing to a settee in the middle of the room. They both sat down on it. The countess took a chair across from them.

"The place to start your trip is Rome, of course," the professor began. "I think you and *la bella contessa* should plan on staying in the city for a month at the very least. Then, I would suggest you hire a carriage and make your way north to Siena, Florence, Bologna, then Venice. . . ."

As the elderly gentleman listed all the important sights to be seen in each city, the museums and theaters to visit, the lectures to attend, Belle listened breathlessly, scarcely able to believe that she would soon be standing in the Colosseum and walking across the Bridge of Sighs.

It was almost enough to make her forget about her father. Almost.

The minutes sped by, and then the hours, as the three talked. Mouchard entered the room bearing finger sandwiches on a silver tray. The professor helped himself, but

Belle politely declined. She was too excited by her travel plans to even think about eating.

Completely enraptured by what Professore Truffatore was telling her, Belle didn't notice the countess's expression darken as she refused the food, and was only dimly aware that the countess waved Mouchard to her, whispered something in his ear, and then dismissed him.

Moments later, however, Belle was forced to tear her attention away from the professor, because there was a loud knock on the study door.

Mouchard opened it, stepped inside the room, and announced a newly arrived visitor.

"Your Ladyship . . . Henri, duc des Choses-Passées."

CHAPTER THIRTY

"MONSIEUR HENRI, DARLING BOY! What a pleasure it is to see you again!" the countess exclaimed.

"Madame Comtesse!" Henri, said, striding across the room to take her hand. "And Mademoiselle Belle, too? This is my lucky day!"

He bowed to the ladies, and then the countess introduced him to Professore Truffatore.

"You will be interested to know, Professore, that our young duke here is also a scholar. He's a student at the Sorbonne," the countess said.

Belle inclined her head, impressed. She'd had no idea Henri studied at France's most prestigious university.

"You are enjoying your studies, Monsieur Henri?" the professor asked.

Henri nodded. Proudly, but shyly, too. Belle was touched by his humility.

"Monsieur Henri is studying both economics and science," the countess continued. "He wants to learn how to become a better steward of his land and find ways to help the people of his region prosper."

"That's very admirable," said the professor.

"Not only that, he's at the top of his class," the countess said knowingly. "I happened to be at a dinner with one of his professors recently."

Henri, coloring slightly, looked at the floor. "Madame Comtesse, you are making me blush," he said.

"Nonsense! Your modesty is very becoming, Monsieur Henri, but I wish more sons of the nobility would follow your example. Rogues and wastrels, most of them," the countess sniffed.

Henri laughed. He shot Belle a *Help me!* glance.

"Sit with us, Monsieur Henri!" the countess said. "You must be hungry after your trip. I'll have Mouchard fetch you something to eat."

"I'd love to," Henri said, with a grimace. "But I'm afraid I'm rather dusty from the carriage ride, and I don't want to dirty the furniture," he said. "I'll go and change my clothes, shall I?"

"I have a better idea," the countess said. "Let's walk outside. You can shake the dust off, and we can all stretch our legs." The countess rose from her chair. "Come," she said, taking the professor's arm. "Let's go to the orchard. I want to show off my prize pear trees."

Henri offered Belle his arm, and they followed the countess and professor out of the summer house and across the lawns. Belle was glad to see him. He was funny and smart, and it was nice to have someone of her own age to talk with.

"You look so lovely today, Belle," he observed. "Have you had a nice morning with the countess?"

"Thank you, Henri," said Belle. "I have had a nice morning. We've spent it planning a trip to Italy. I'm so excited, I can't even tell you. It's something wonderful to look forward to, of course, and it also . . ." She hesitated. "Well, it . . . it takes my mind off things."

Henri looked at her, his forehead furrowed with concern. "What things, Belle?" he asked.

"My . . . my situation," Belle said, wishing she could take her words back and turn the conversation from the morose direction it was taking.

It was all the fault of the music boxes. They'd reminded her of her father. And now she was desperate to tell someone about her feelings. To pour her heart out to a friend.

"The thing is . . . well, it's my father. I—I haven't seen him for quite some time. And I used to see him *all* the time. And I—oh, Henri, I *miss* him so much," she said, squeezing Henri's arm. And then she couldn't say any more, because of the giant lump in her throat.

Henri covered her hand with his own. "You don't have to explain, Belle. I understand. I know it's been hard for you lately," he said.

Belle nodded, grateful that he'd listened, and grateful that he was doing the talking now so she didn't have to.

"I must confess that I didn't come up to the country only to see the countess. I was hoping you'd be here, too," he said. "I've missed you, Belle. It's not every day that I make a friend who can rattle off *Hamlet* in its entirety."

"I doubt that very much," Belle said, in control of her emotions again. "You're a duke, Henri. You live in Paris. I bet you have dozens of friends, and I bet they're all terribly clever and entertaining."

Henri gazed off into the distance. "Yes, they are," he said with a sigh. "That's the problem. My life . . . so much of it is nothing but dances and parties, hounds and horses."

"That sounds truly dreadful," Belle teased. "How do you stand it?"

Henri reddened. He smiled bashfully. "I sound like a twit, don't I? Who complains about parties?" His smile dimmed. "It's just that sometimes . . ." His voice trailed off.

"What?" Belle asked.

He met her eyes. "Sometimes it's nice *not* to have to say clever things. Sometimes it's nice to have a friend with whom I can be myself and talk about things that really matter. Like Shakespeare. Or school. Or things that trouble me, like the future of my estate."

His eyes were warm and deep, and Belle felt as if they could see inside of her—straight to her heart. Like the truest of friends could.

"Or like fathers whom you never see," she said, holding his gaze. "Because you live in an enchanted castle where it snows all the time. With a strange, unknowable beast. And talking teapots. And roses slowly dying under heavy glass cloches."

Henri nodded. "Yes. Or that. I struggle with that a lot," he assured her.

Belle gave him a sidelong look. "I'm *serious*, Henri."

"I am, too!" Henri said. But Belle could tell he was teasing her. "I have the same problems in *my* enchanted castle, only worse," he insisted. "My chamberpot talks. All night long. It dances, too, often when I'm trying to use it. Very inconvenient, let me tell you."

Belle burst into laughter. "Why do I even talk to you? You're horrible!" she said.

"It's true, I *am*," Henri admitted with a grin. "But I got you to laugh, Belle. And that's half the battle with one's troubles—learning to laugh at them. You looked so sad a moment ago, I couldn't bear it. Now you're smiling again."

Belle's smile deepened. It was so nice sharing her feelings with someone who shared his, too. It made a change from the Beast, who refused to ever share his feelings.

"I think of you as my friend, Belle," Henri said. "And I hope you consider me yours. And friends are there for each other no matter what, good or bad."

"I do, Henri. Thank you," Belle said.

"Belle! Monsieur Henri! Where are you?" a voice shouted.

It was the countess. She and the professor were already in the orchard. Belle and Henri were almost among the trees themselves; Belle hadn't realized how far they'd walked.

"Coming!" Henri shouted back.

Belle looked at the rows of perfectly pruned, glossy-leaved pear trees. There wasn't a dead limb, a spot of blight, or a patch of rot to be seen on any of them. It was unlike any

any orchard she'd ever been in. It was perfect and lovely, like everything else in *Nevermore*.

Henri offered her his hand. "Let's find them. And maybe a pear, too, while we're at it," he said. "I'm starving."

But Belle hesitated. "Henri?" she said tentatively.

"Mmm?"

"It's strange, this place. *Nevermore*. Don't you think so?"

Henri raised an eyebrow. "And your enchanted castle situation . . . that's perfectly normal?"

"Hardly," Belle conceded. "But that's not this . . ." She gestured at the lush gardens behind them, the perfect orchard in front of them. "This is all so pretty, so perfect. *Too* perfect. Sometimes I'm afraid it won't last. That it can't last. I'm afraid I'll try to come back to it one day, and it won't be here anymore. I keep reminding myself that it's not real. But I *want* it to be, so badly."

"Monsieur Henri! Belle! Come and get a pear! Quickly, before the professor eats every single one in the orchard!" the countess trilled.

She sounded farther away now. Belle could just glimpse her black dress through the trees, and the deep russet of the professor's jacket.

"Coming!" Henri called to her. "Come on, Belle, let's go.

184

Forget your worries. You're here with us. Right now. With friends who care about you. Nothing's more real than that."

And then he dashed into the orchard, shouting to the countess that he would find the best, most perfect pear of all.

Belle decided to take Henri's advice. She would forget her worries. At least for now. Smiling, she ran after him. He'd gotten a head start on her and was nowhere to be found. Neither was the countess, or the professor.

She heard an exultant shout, then laughter.

"Henri?" she called. "Madame Comtesse?"

No one answered, but she saw a flash of movement in the trees just ahead.

"Belle? Where are you?" Henri called.

"Over here!" Belle shouted.

"Monsieur Henri? Professore? Where on earth have you gone?"

That was the countess.

They were all lost in the orchard now.

Belle hurried toward the trees where she'd glimpsed someone moving. She soon discovered that it was a woman, but it was not the countess. The handle of a basket was looped over her arm. She was wearing a serviceable white linen dress with a white pinafore. On her head was a plain straw hat. In her hand was a pair of silver fruit scissors. As Belle watched, the woman snipped a pear from a tree and caught it in her basket.

She must be one of the countess's servants, Belle thought. *She's probably picking pears for the cook.*

"Hello!" Belle said as she drew close to her.

The servant turned. She raised her face to Belle's.

Belle took a stumbling step backward. Her hands clenched into fists.

White clothing. Silvery hair.

It was the madwoman.

CHAPTER THIRTY-ONE

"BELLE? CHILD, where are you?" the countess shouted.

"I'm over here, my lady!" Belle yelled back, her eyes trained on the madwoman . . . and the sharp scissors she was holding.

"She's nearby," Belle warned. "They're all nearby. If I scream, they'll come running."

The madwoman cast a wary glance in the countess's directions, then put a finger to her lips. Belle sucked in her breath, not sure if she should stay where she was or run. If she ran, she would have to turn her back on the woman. And turning her back on someone holding a pair of scissors, even small ones, didn't seem like a smart thing to do.

The madwoman stopped. She held out her basket, then put it on the ground. "Look, child!" she urged.

Belle peered into it, expecting to see freshly picked pears. Instead, she saw pomegranates.

With a shiver, Belle recalled that they were the food of the dead. Hades had tricked Persephone into eating them so that he could keep her with him in the underworld.

"Belle? Have you tried a pear yet?" The countess's voice was louder. She was closer.

The madwoman cast another glance, this one frantic, in the countess's direction. She was still holding her silver scissors. All at once, she lunged at Belle.

Belle had no time to scream.

But instead of plunging the scissors into her, as Belle feared, the madwoman grabbed her hand, put the scissors into them, and closed her fingers over them.

"Keep them! Hide them!" she urged, her eyes large in her face.

Belle stood frozen.

"Did you hear me, girl? Put them in your pocket!" the madwoman demanded.

Belle, unnerved, did as she was told.

The madwoman backed away, her finger to her lips, her

gaze on the approaching countess. She looked at Belle one last time, a heart-wrenching sadness in her eyes, then she turned and ran.

She disappeared through the trees like the morning mist, and Belle, who was still holding her breath, finally let it out.

CHAPTER THIRTY-TWO

"THERE YOU ARE!" the countess said to Belle. Henri was with her. "My word, child, how flushed you look! Is anything wrong?"

"No," Belle said, forcing a smile. "Nothing at all. I was . . . I was running and got a bit winded, that's all."

Belle surprised herself with her denial. She'd been about to tell the countess of her run-in with the madwoman, but the memory of the woman's eyes—the look of desperate sadness in them—stopped her. The madwoman had held a finger to her lips. She had not wanted the countess to learn of her presence.

Why? And why had she handed Belle scissors and told

her to hide them? Why had she stolen the hat full of coins from the little boy at the Palais-Royal?

"Monsieur Henri, you ran too fast for Belle!" the countess scolded. "She's a young lady, not a racehorse!"

But Henri didn't hear the countess. He was looking up into a tree. The professor joined him, and they both marveled at its heavily laden branches bent under the weight of hundreds of golden pears kissed with blushes of pink. The fruits' perfume, with its rich notes of vanilla and honey, was intoxicating.

"I'll find you a perfect one, Belle," Henri said.

The madwoman's basket was on the ground where she'd left it. Belle peered into it again. It was full of pears, not pomegranates.

Am I losing my mind, too? she wondered.

"Here you go!"

It was Henri. He was at her side now, offering her a flawless pear.

Belle took it. The madwoman's creatures had warned her against eating anything in *Nevermore*. Yet she'd eaten a sweet at the ball, and another at the Palais-Royal, and she'd been perfectly fine. Nothing had happened to her. They'd warned her against leaving things in *Nevermore*, too, but she *hadn't* left anything here.

"Try it, Belle, do," the countess said, joining them. "I grew these trees myself. Fussed over them ever since they were saplings."

Belle looked at the pear, so heavy in her hand, so perfect, so enticing.

"You *must* sample one, Belle! You've never tasted anything so delicious," the professor said, biting into one. "I'm on my second!"

"Actually, that's your *fourth*, Professore!" the countess said, laughing as juice ran down his chin.

Belle glanced at Henri.

"I will if you will," he said, a challenge in his eyes.

He's my friend, Belle thought. *He wouldn't encourage me to do anything dangerous.*

They both took bites at the same time. The pear's flesh was yielding and sweet; at first Belle loved the taste, but it soon became cloying, and the orchard's perfume dizzying.

"What do you think? I'm right! They are superior. Tell me, Belle, have you ever had the like?"

"Never, my lady," Belle replied, not wanting to be rude. She forced herself to finish the pear and threw the core into the grass. Henri picked another and ate it, but Belle couldn't.

As she watched Henri, the countess, and the professor enjoying their pears, a lassitude descended on her. Her limbs felt heavy, her mind dull. She felt as if she could lie down under a tree and sleep forever.

Was it the pear that had made her feel this way? She tried to recall the beetle's words. There was a warning in them, but its meaning eluded her. Something eaten, something beaten? Was that it? Or was it *not* eaten and *not* beaten? Did it really matter? It was so hard to think, so exhausting. It was much easier to let others do it for you.

"Darling Belle, you look absolutely exhausted. Would you like to have a rest?" the countess asked.

Belle said that she would. Professore Truffatore, who was evidently not tired at all, declared that he wished to see the countess's apple trees. It was decided that Henri would accompany him and that the countess would walk Belle back to the summer house to show her to a room where she could lie down.

"I might rest, too," the countess said as she and Belle walked out of the orchard. "A little nap before dinner sounds like just the thing."

Dinner!

Belle's heart lurched. She was suddenly wide awake. Chip's party! It was to take place after dinner that very night.

And she had forgotten all about it.

CHAPTER THIRTY-THREE

"MY LADY," BELLE SAID, panicking, "forgive me, but I have to leave right away!"

She had promised to be at Chip's party. She'd given the decorations she'd made to Mrs. Potts earlier in the day but was supposed to help hang them. Could she make it back in time, or was it too late? How long had she been in *Nevermore*?

"Leave? Whatever for?" the countess asked, dismayed.

Belle explained.

When she finished, the countess gave her a look. "I see. You're going to a party. For a piece of porcelain," she said. "When you could be here with your friends. Your *true* friends."

"Chip is my friend, too. And his mother. They'll be heartbroken if I'm not there. Please understand, Madame Comtesse. I owe them that."

"Nonsense!" the countess said vehemently. "You don't owe anyone in the Beast's castle anything!"

There was an anger in her voice that Belle had never heard before, and it startled her. But it was gone as quickly as it had come.

"Forgive me, child," said the countess silkily. "My emotion got the better of me. I can't bear to see a young woman constrained so, or her dear . . . or an old friend in dire—" She stopped suddenly, as if she'd said too much. "Mouchard!" she barked, motioning to him. "Ready a carriage for Mademoiselle Belle."

Something about the countess's words struck Belle. "Pardon me, my lady, but what was that about an old friend?" she asked.

"It's nothing," the countess said, waving Belle's concern away.

But Belle would not be put off. She knew that she herself was the *young woman constrained*, but the *her dear* and *old friend* troubled her. There was one person who was both dear to Belle and an old friend of the countess's.

"Madame Comtesse, were you speaking of my father?" asked Belle, fear plucking at her nerves. "If there's something wrong, you must tell me. *Please.*"

The countess heaved a troubled sigh. "Very well. Your father and I—we've been acquainted for some time. I haven't seen him in ages, but I went to visit him yesterday. I was worried."

Belle's eyes widened. "You saw my father?" she said, her voice barely a whisper. "How is he?"

The countess put a steadying hand on Belle's arm. "He's aged, Belle. He's slower. A little confused at times. It's sorrow, I believe. And guilt. Guilt over the fact that you took his place in the Beast's castle. It's eating him alive."

Belle was not one to cry easily, but at the countess's words, tears welled in her eyes. "If only I could *do* something," she said anxiously.

"Hush, child. Don't cry. I wouldn't have told you any of this if I didn't think there was a way to help him," said the countess.

Belle clutched the countess's hand, hope leaping in her heart. "What is it?" she asked.

"I intend to bring your father to *Nevermore.*"

CHAPTER THIRTY-FOUR

BELLE COULD NOT BELIEVE what she'd just heard.

"My lady," she said, her voice barely a whisper. "You could do that? You could bring my father *here*?"

"I can *try*," the countess said. "In fact, I've been trying. As yet I haven't succeeded. My powers are strong, Belle, but they are not unlimited."

"But you brought *me* here," Belle said, a pleading note in her voice. She had resigned herself to the fact that she would never see her beloved father again, but now the countess had told her that she had a chance to, and Belle wanted that chance. More than she'd ever wanted anything in her life.

"Yes, I did bring you here," the countess allowed. "But

that's because the magic in the Beast's castle augments my own and makes it possible for you to walk in and out of this world through an enchanted book. But Villeneuve . . ." She smiled tartly. "Well, let's just say there is not much magic in *that* place."

Belle's face fell.

"Do not give up hope, child. I will keep trying."

"I would be so grateful if I could see my father once again, Madame Comtesse. It would mean the world to me."

"I want you to do more than just see him, Belle."

Belle looked at her questioningly.

"I want you and your father to stay here. With me. Forever."

"But that's impossible. *Nevermore* isn't real."

"It can be. There is a way. Trust me. Let *me* be the author of your story, not the Beast."

A feeling of hopelessness descended on Belle. She wanted what the countess was offering so badly, but she knew she couldn't have it.

"Even if *Nevermore* could become a reality, I still couldn't stay here forever," she said. "I exchanged my freedom for my father's. What's done cannot be undone."

The countess cupped Belle's cheek. "Do not be so certain, child," she said. "I have undone much in my time, and many."

There was a fierceness to her voice, and it chilled Belle, but it also gave her resolve. Perhaps there *was* a way for her to live in *Nevermore* with her father. She wanted so much to believe that there was.

As if sensing her thoughts, the countess said, "Believe in me, Belle."

Belle nodded her head. "I will, my lady."

"Will?" the countess said, arching an eyebrow.

"I *do*," said Belle, mustering a smile.

The countess smiled, too. Belle hugged her and thanked her, then ran down the steps to the waiting carriage. Mouchard handed her up and closed the door behind her. The driver cracked the whip and his horses picked up a trot. Half an hour later, Belle was back at the château.

Mouchard's expression, as always, was as somber as a tombstone as he helped her out of the carriage. He nodded as she thanked him, then closed the door and took his seat once more. The carriage rolled off toward the stables. Dusk had fallen during the return ride, and Belle stood alone in it now without so much as a candle to light her way.

As her eyes adjusted, she made her way up the drive to the portal once again. The yew trees had grown even higher during the few hours she had been in the country. They'd formed themselves into narrow, mazelike passageways.

Gnarled, knobby roots snaked across the ground now, too, forcing Belle to choose her steps carefully.

She had just started down one of them when she heard it—a rustling.

Unnerved, Belle picked up her pace. She tried to tell herself it was only a mouse or some other tiny night creature scampering to its den, but it grew louder and more insistent. She stopped and held her breath, the better to listen.

"Hello? Who's there?" she called out, her voice trembling almost as hard as her legs were.

The rustling seemed to be not behind her or ahead of her, but all around her.

Belle's stomach pitched with fear as she realized it was the sound of branches and canes, limbs and stalks. The rosebushes, the yew trees . . . they were growing so fast, she could hear them.

Hurry! a voice inside her urged. *Get to the book!*

With a cry, Belle ran toward it. Then something grabbed hold of her foot. Pain shot up her leg. She tumbled forward, hitting the ground hard.

Belle looked down at her foot, terrified of what she might see. A tree root was twisted around her ankle like a sea monster's tentacle. She kicked at it with her other foot. It released her and shrank back into the ground. Belle tried to scramble up, but the thorns caught hold of her sleeve. She tore her arm free and ran to the book, desperate to step through its pages to safety.

The shimmering silver reminded her of ice in a pond in December—not fully solid or liquid. She pushed her way through and stumbled out into the library's small workroom, her breath coming in short gasps.

Belle turned and saw the book looming behind her. Hands shaking, she slammed it shut and backed away. The thorny branches, the twisted roots—she half expected them to come snaking out of the pages after her, but the book merely shrank back to its normal size, and Belle hid it in the desk drawer once again.

As she closed the drawer, a sudden volley of knocking made her jump. It was emanating from the library's outer doors.

"I'm coming!" she shouted, hurrying out of the workroom.

"There you are, Belle!" Lumiere said, as she opened the library's doors. "Are you ready? Dinner's just about to be served, and . . . my goodness, but it's dark in here! How do you see anything?"

He walked to a tall candelabrum standing on a table and lit its tapers.

"That's better! Now listen, Belle. . . . The master's in on the surprise, too. Dinner's nearly ready. You should see the cake Cuisinier made! We're going to . . . Belle?" He paused again, peering at her closely. "What's wrong?" he asked, his flames flaring. "You look like you've seen a ghost."

Belle forced a smile. "The knocking startled me, that's all," she said. "I'll be right down, Lumiere. I just need to change my clothes."

Lumiere nodded. He explained the rest of the plan to Belle, then hurried out of the library and down the stairs. As he did, Belle pressed a hand to her chest, trying to calm her thumping heart.

The walk through from the château to the portal had scared her badly. The branches and roots—it almost seemed as if they'd been reaching for her, as if they'd wanted to wrap themselves around her and pull her deep within themselves where no one could see her struggle or hear her scream.

"Stop it," she said aloud. "You're being silly. The hedges were a little overgrown, that's all. You let your imagination run wild and scared yourself."

But Belle knew that wasn't true.

"*Nevermore* wants me," she whispered aloud. "It wants me to stay."

The thought scared her.

But what scared her even more was how much she wanted *Nevermore.*

CHAPTER THIRTY-FIVE

HENRI STOOD AT A WINDOW in Death's study, gazing out of it at her rose gardens.

Professore Truffatore sat on the leather settee, a book open in his lap, a pear in his hand.

All around the study—on the mantel, the bookshelves, the top of tables—vultures perched. One rested atop Death's forearm as she paced the study, his powerful talons gripping her flesh tightly.

"It's worse than I thought, Mouchard. Belle actually *cares* for that ridiculous little teacup. Why, she even left *Nevermore* for him!" Death said, stroking the bird's black feathers. "She has feelings for *all* the servants now. *And* the Beast. She tries to befriend him, no matter how badly he behaves. And he tries, too! One day, one of them might do more than try. They might actually succeed."

The vulture turned his beady eyes to Death and squawked.

"I know, Mouchard, I know. I *can't* have that. Not at all," Death fumed, scratching the bird's bald head. "I'm playing my last card, my trump card, and it *has* to work. Belle is starting to doubt *Nevermore*. I can see it in her eyes. But she wants to be with her father so much, her heart overrules her doubts. For *now*, at least, but not for much longer."

A vulture perched on the mantel stretched his wings out and screeched.

"You're right, Truqué. She *is* almost bound to *Nevermore*. If all goes well, one more visit will do the trick." Death smiled slyly. "And then *I* win the wager."

With a wave of her free hand, she summoned her entire flock. "Come, my darlings. We have work to do."

Mouchard flew off her arm, and Truqué launched himself off the mantel. Death left the room in a rustle of black silk, her vultures flapping behind her.

The professor remained on the leather settee.

And Henri continued to gaze out of the window.

Perfectly, impossibly, still.

CHAPTER THIRTY-SIX

"IS HE COMING? He's not back yet, is he?" Mrs. Potts whispered.

"Don't worry, Mrs. Potts. He's nowhere in sight," Belle said, peering out a kitchen window.

"Is everything ready?"

"It is," Belle assured her. "As soon as I see him, I'll run back to the dining room to get everyone ready, just as we planned."

Belle had come down to dinner, and she and the Beast had eaten their meal in the dining room as they did on most evenings. They'd hurried through this one, though. The Beast had been far too excited for Chip's party to linger over Cuisinier's *boeuf bourguignon*.

As soon as the dishes had been cleared, Mrs. Potts had asked her son to check that the doors to the stables and the chicken coop were locked up tightly for the night. The second he left the kitchen, she'd raced back into the dining room to give the signal. Everyone had snapped into action.

The Beast had quickly hung the colorful garlands that Belle had made all around the dining room. One spelled out HAPPY BIRTHDAY, CHIP!

Chapeau had carried the birthday cake from its hiding place in a kitchen cupboard to the dining room table. Lumiere had followed him with plates and cutlery, and Belle had fetched the presents from a cabinet in the scullery.

"Here he comes!" she whisper-shouted now.

She ran out of the kitchen and into the dining room, shutting the door behind her, then pressed her ear to the keyhole.

Chip came into the kitchen, shaking snow off himself.

"Is the barn secure? No weasels can get into the chicken coop?" Mrs. Potts asked.

"Everything's locked up tight," Chip said. He looked around the empty kitchen. "Where is everyone, Mama?" he asked.

"They've all gone to bed for the night. Everyone was tired, I guess. I offered to finish up the dishes. Why, love? Is something the matter?"

"I thought . . ." Chip began. "Well, since it's my birthday, I thought we could all . . . oh, never mind," he said dejectedly.

Mrs. Potts gave him a sympathetic smile. "Grown-ups don't always remember youngsters' birthdays, but you and I can stay up and celebrate with some nice stories by the fire, can't we?"

Chip nodded. He mustered a smile. He was far too good a child to whine or complain.

"Before we do, though," Mrs. Potts continued, "would you check the dining room to make sure all the plates have been brought in?"

"Yes, Mama," Chip said.

Belle peered through the keyhole and saw him making his way toward her, his sweet face downcast. Froufrou was right behind him. Chip didn't know it, but his mother was, too.

Belle dashed away from the door. "He's coming!" she whispered, joining the others, who were by the cake.

Lumiere quickly lit the candles. He finished just as Chip opened the door.

"Surprise!" everyone yelled.

The look of utter happiness on Chip's face lit up the room.

"Happy birthday, Chip!" Lumiere shouted, and the whole room burst into song.

When they'd finished, Cogsworth said, "Now come, young man, and blow the candles out before they light the draperies on fire and burn the castle down!"

"Make a wish first!" said Mrs. Potts, throwing Cogsworth a look.

Chip closed his eyes. He thought for a few seconds, then said, "I wish to always have my mama, and Belle, and my other friends, and the master around me, and to be as happy as I am right now!" And then he blew his candles out with one breath.

Everyone applauded and smiled at Chip's words, but Belle saw a hint of sorrow behind the smiles. It was as if his wish had brought back thoughts of happier times—times he was too young to remember.

As the smoke from the birthday candles rose into the air, Lumiere clapped his candle hands together as if to dispel the sad memories. "Well, now! I think I spy a present or two!" he said.

With a whoop of delight, Chip dove into the pile.

There was a warm quilt from Mrs. Potts, and a nightcap that Belle had stitched just yesterday. Froufrou contributed a well-chewed, half-frozen bone dug up outside. Lumiere and Cogsworth provided pirate accessories, including a tricorn hat and a red scarf they'd found in the attic. Plumette gave Chip a gold hoop earring, which she hung from his handle. And from the Beast, there was a beautifully carved wooden chest with brass clasps and hinges.

"What's in it, master?" Chip asked excitedly.

"Open it and see," said the Beast, smiling.

Chapeau eased the heavy lid back. A hushed "Oh!" went up as everyone saw what the chest contained: magnificent model ships. There were five fully rigged warships, four merchant vessels, and six brigantines flying the skull and crossbones. There were also painted figures of officers, sailors, and pirates to man the ships, and an enormous map of the world, hand-painted on linen, to sail them upon.

"It's no fun being a pirate without a few merchant ships to plunder and some warships to outrun," said the Beast.

Chip, staring at the chest and its contents as if dazed, was speechless.

"Chip, your manners!" Mrs. Potts whispered to her son.

Chip looked up at the Beast. "Thank you, master! Oh, *thank* you!" he said.

"You're very welcome, lad."

"They're so handsome. Where did they come from?" Chip asked.

"They were mine," the Beast replied. "I spent many happy hours playing with them. A long time ago. I hope you will, too."

Belle cut slices of cake for herself and the Beast, and Mrs. Potts poured two cups of tea. Only Belle and the Beast ate. The enchanted servants, objects all, needed no food.

The Beast, meanwhile, watched Chip and Cogsworth pull the map out, smooth it open on the floor, and position the ships across it. Lumiere and Plumette watched, laughing, as they launched into a noisy battle—Chip manning the brigantines, and Cogsworth the warships.

"Why, this brings back the time we cavalrymen watched from the shore as the French navy engaged Admiral Hawke at the Battle of Quiberon Bay during the Seven Years' War!" Cogsworth declared.

"That's absolutely riveting, Cogsworth," said Lumiere. "Now watch out, before that brig blasts you!"

As Belle was eating her cake, Mrs. Potts came up to her. "Thank you, Belle. Thank you so much for making him so happy."

"It was nothing, Mrs. Potts. Really," Belle said.

"To my son and to me, it's everything," Mrs. Potts said, a catch in her voice. She bustled off to refresh the tea cups.

Unbeknownst to Belle, the Beast caught her exchange with

Mrs. Potts. He bowed his head, then quietly excused himself. Belle, turning to put her empty plate and fork down, didn't see him go. She didn't see him turn back in the doorway, and gaze at Chip, and then Mrs. Potts, with a look of anguish in his eyes.

Cogsworth and Chip continued the naval battle. Chapeau cleared the plates. Froufrou curled up by the fire. And Lumiere and Plumette made eyes at each other. Eventually, Mrs. Potts declared that it was getting late. Chip thanked everyone, and then his mother bustled him off to bed. Plumette and Cogsworth cleared up, and Belle put the ships back into the chest.

As she was folding up the map, she realized the Beast was gone. Disappointment settled over her. She'd been looking forward to talking to him about the party—telling him what an amazing gift he'd given Chip; asking him if he liked the cake; reliving a fun event after it had ended, as friends did. But he'd left. *Again.*

"What a lovely party," Lumiere said as he closed the top of the chest. Then he looked into Belle's eyes and said, "And it's all because of you, Belle. You bring brightness and hope to this gloomy castle. Not only for Chip, though he loves you dearly—but for all of us."

"*Most* of you, you mean," Belle said ruefully. "I'm sure the

Beast doesn't feel that I bring him brightness, hope, or much of anything at all."

"Belle, that's not true," Lumiere said fervently. "Your friendship means a great deal to him. I know it does."

Belle shook her head. She thought of the countess, and Henri, and the easy way she had with each of them. "But friends talk, Lumiere," she said. "They share confidences. They trust each other, even with difficult things—*especially* with difficult things."

"Sometimes, Belle, our troubles are too deep for words," Lumiere said. "It's at times like those when we need our friends the most."

"Lumiere! Can you come? Chapeau opened the kitchen door and the wind blew all the candles out. We need you to relight them!"

It was Plumette, calling from the kitchen.

"Never a dull moment around here. Good night, Belle," he said.

"Good night, Lumiere."

Belle left the dining room and made her way upstairs to her room. She washed her face, brushed her teeth, and changed into her nightgown, but instead of getting right into bed, she sat in the window seat and looked out at the snowy night.

CHAPTER THIRTY-SIX

Never had she felt so torn.

Lumiere said that Chip and the others cared for her, that she made them happy. He said that even the Beast valued her friendship, and that he needed her. But how could that be? All she did was make him angry or sad. How many times had he walked out on her when the discussion took a turn he didn't like? How many times had she asked him for answers, only to be left with more questions?

The Beast was a creature filled with sadness, haunted by a pain Belle didn't understand and couldn't name. Life with him was like the endless winter outside her window, with no hope of spring.

Nevermore, however, promised her an endless summer. People were fascinating. Life was beautiful. *Everything* was beautiful. The countess and Henri and the professor were there, and they clearly wanted the best for her.

And if the countess's magic succeeded, her father would be there, too. And he needed her more than anyone.

Belle watched as the snow came down, the heavy white flakes swirling through the black night.

If she left the Beast's castle, if the countess found a way out for her, Belle knew she would break Chip's heart. And Mrs. Potts's. Maybe the other servants' hearts, too. Maybe even the Beast's.

But if she stayed, and missed the chance to be reunited with her father, she would break her own.

"What do I do?" she whispered to the darkness.

But the darkness gave her no answer.

CHAPTER THIRTY-SEVEN

COGSWORTH, HOLDING a wooden ladle, served Belle and the Beast their morning oatmeal.

As he bent toward Belle, his hand shook, then stiffened.

"Oh, dear. Oh, my," he said. "A sticky gear. I shall have to oil it."

Lumiere looked up from the hearth, where he was trying to coax life into the sputtering fire.

Chapeau sped to Cogsworth's rescue, taking the ladle from him and setting it down, then giving his arm a good rub.

"Ah! Much better. Thank you, old man," Cogsworth said.

He reached for the ladle again, ready to resume his duties,

but as he did, a terrible grinding was heard. A groan escaped him. His hands went to the small of his back.

The Beast, concerned, glanced first at Cogsworth, then at Lumiere. He expected to see cheerful exasperation on Lumiere's face, or hear a teasing comment. Instead he saw a look of profound sorrow. It broke his heart.

Things were getting worse every day for his servants; he could see it. Soon, their movements would become even stiffer. Then their ability to move and speak would cease. The light would go out of their eyes. They would become lifeless candlesticks, clocks, teapots . . . forever.

"If you would pardon us a moment, master," Lumiere said.

"An old war injury," said Cogsworth apologetically. "Acquired during the Battle of Hastenbeck alongside my old friend, général Chevert. We were to drive out the Hanoverians, you see, but the devils were dug in—"

"Is that so?" said Lumiere. "Come into the kitchen, *mon ami*. I'm sure Cuisinier is dying to hear all about it. . . ."

The Beast watched Cogsworth hobble off with Lumiere's protective arm around him. He glanced at Belle to see if she'd noticed. She hadn't. She was gazing at her oatmeal. Not eating it, just listlessly stirring it with her spoon.

Normally, another's distress would have shaken Belle

from the torpor she was in. Today, however, it seemed only to deepen it. Something was wrong—very wrong. The Beast could feel it.

"Why aren't you eating, Belle? Are you not well?" he asked.

"I'm fine, thank you. Just not terribly hungry," Belle said, giving him what was clearly a fake smile. She laid her spoon down. "I didn't sleep well last night. In fact, if you'll excuse me, I'll take my leave."

The Beast raised an eyebrow. "Where are you going?"

"To the library."

"Would you like to go for a walk through the grounds instead? The brisk air will put some color back into your cheeks. You look so pale this morning. Surely you've noticed."

"How could I?" Belle asked. "There aren't any mirrors here."

"True."

"Because you broke them all."

The Beast cleared his throat. "Also true," he said. "Personally? I like books better than mirrors," he added, trying to lighten the mood. "Mirrors only show us what we are. Books show us what we can be."

"I agree completely," said Belle. "Which is why I'm going to the library."

"But Belle, the servants . . . they tell me you're in there all day. Don't you think a bit of balance is needed? An escape can become escapism before we even know it. Books are wonderful things, but you can't live in someone else's story. You have to live your own story."

Belle looked up at him with deep pain in her eyes. What she said next broke his heart for the second time that morning.

"But what if you don't like your story? What then?"

CHAPTER THIRTY-EIGHT

BELLE WAITED FOR AN ANSWER from the Beast.

But as usual, it didn't come. He had put his spoon down, a stricken look on his face, but he didn't speak.

Belle felt a familiar frustration rise inside her. She told herself that soon the Beast's unwillingness to talk to her wouldn't matter. She was going to *Nevermore* today. It was quite possible that she would not be coming back.

But as she sat looking at the creature she'd tried so hard to befriend, she decided that there was something *she* wanted to say before she left.

"You know, one question haunts me more than all the

rest. Do you remember that night when you found me in the West Wing? After you'd told me not to go there?"

The Beast broke her gaze. He looked out of the window. It was snowing. Still. The wind moaned, swirling white flakes through the castle's turrets and towers.

"The night you ran away?" he said at length. "And nearly got yourself killed by a pack of wolves? That night? Yes, I do seem to recall it."

"The wolves nearly killed you, too. You managed to drive them off, but they wounded you badly. You collapsed in the snow. Philippe and I got you back to the castle."

"I know this already, Belle. I have the scars to remind me."

"What you don't know is that I looked at you while you were lying on the ground. Unconscious. Your blood seeping into the snow. And I almost didn't help you. Because a voice inside me was shouting, 'Run! Hurry! This is your chance to escape!'"

"But you didn't run."

"I couldn't. You were helpless. Defenseless. I would've been leaving you to die."

The Beast turned from the window and met her eyes. "Why are we doing this, Belle? Why are we reliving such an awful night?"

"Because even though I didn't get all the answers I wanted that night, I still learned something. Do you know what it is?"

The Beast shook his head.

"I found out that you were willing to die for me, and that I wasn't willing to let you." She laughed sadly.

A silence fell then. It was like a wall between them, hard and impenetrable. The Beast was the first to break through it.

"I have something for you, Belle. It's only a small thing. I came across it last night. In a drawer in my study. I thought you might like it."

"You're changing the subject," Belle said.

"I'm certainly trying," said the Beast, with the hint of a smile.

"What is it?" Belle asked.

The Beast stood. He walked to Belle, pulled something out of his coat pocket, and handed it to her. Belle saw that it was a glass heart dangling from a gold chain. The heart was cut so that it sparkled with light no matter which way she turned it.

"It belonged to my mother," the Beast said.

"It's truly beautiful. But I can't take it. It should stay in your family," Belle said, trying to hand it back.

But the Beast shook his head. "I want you to have it."

"Would you put it on for me?" Belle asked.

The Beast shook his head. He held up his large, clumsy paws.

Belle fastened it around her neck herself.

"It suits you," the Beast said.

"Tell me about her."

"She was smart. Beautiful. Graceful. And kind. The kindest creature I have ever met." He raised his eyes to Belle's. "Well, one of them."

Belle's eyes sought the Beast's. "Why, Beast? What does this mean?"

The Beast looked away.

Belle held her hands up, resigned. "I know, I know," she said wearily. "You can't tell me that."

The Beast looked at her for a long moment. Then, with the saddest smile Belle had ever seen, he said, "I just *did* tell you something, Belle."

"I don't understand," Belle said.

The Beast nodded at the heart hanging from her neck.

Belle looked down at it. She closed her hand around it. When she looked up again, the Beast was gone.

What did he mean by that? she wondered.

Had she missed something in their conversation? There were so many things he hadn't told her.

CHAPTER THIRTY-EIGHT

And now, she realized, there was something she'd never get to tell him.

"Good-bye," she whispered.

Then she rose and made her way to the library.

CHAPTER THIRTY-NINE

FOR ONCE, Belle beat Mouchard to the door.

She was out of the carriage in a flash, before he'd even jumped down from his seat. She raced up the staircase to the summer house, taking the steps two at a time.

The countess met her inside the foyer.

"My father . . . is he—" Belle started to say.

The countess answered her with a smile.

Belle's hands came up to her mouth. She shook her head, not able to believe her good fortune. Her father was here. *He was here!*

"Where is he?" she asked.

"He was sitting in the gazebo with his sketchpad and pencils, but I believe he's now on the terrace, admiring my roses."

Belle ran across the foyer, deliriously happy. But then she stopped dead and turned around, an anxious expression on her face.

"What's wrong, Belle?" the countess asked.

"I'm . . . I'm almost *afraid* to go to him," Belle replied. "I almost don't want to see him, because I'll only have to leave him again."

"You may not have to leave him, child," said the countess.

"Is that . . . is it *possible?*" asked Belle, not daring to hope.

"I'm *very* close to making it so," said the countess.

"Truly? I'll be able to stay here?" Belle exclaimed. She ran back to the countess and took one of her hands. "My lady, how did you bring this about?"

"Later, my child, later. There will be time to explain everything after you've seen your father."

Belle released the countess's hand, ready to dash off again, but the countess tightened her grip, stopping her.

"Darling girl, wait. . . ."

"What is it? What's wrong?" Belle asked, worried by her cautioning tone.

"He doesn't know you've come. I didn't tell him in case you . . . well, in case you changed your mind. I didn't want to break his heart. I only told him he was coming to a magical place. You will be a surprise to him, Belle. He may be startled. It might be wise to proceed gently," she advised.

Belle's own heart swelled with gratitude. She had never met anyone so totally unselfish, so thoughtful, so *good*.

The countess finally released Belle's hand, but instead of racing off, Belle threw her arms around her neck and kissed her alabaster cheek.

"You are so kind," she said, her voice husky with emotion. "To me. To my father. I will never be able to repay you for all that you've done for us."

"Go, child," the countess said, patting Belle's back. "Go to your father. He's just through there." She broke the embrace and pointed at a pair of doors that led out to the terrace.

Belle raced across the foyer and dashed through the doors.

The foyer had several inner doorways, too, all leading to different parts of the summer house. As Belle's footsteps faded, a figure stepped out of one of them and joined the countess.

"You found a way," Henri said.

The countess laughed. "I've had a way all along . . . *my* way. Let them have a bit of time alone, then go to them.

CHAPTER THIRTY-NINE

Nevermore needs two more things. See that they are given. Do not fail me."

Henri bowed, then left the foyer.

The countess watched him go, her green eyes glittering, a smile on her bloodred lips.

CHAPTER FORTY

BELLE STOOD ON THE TERRACE, her hands clenched.

Her father was only a few feet away from her. He had his back to her and was bending down to admire a white rose.

She couldn't believe her eyes. Was he actually *here*? Was he real?

"*Papa?*" she called.

Maurice froze at the sound of her voice. Then, slowly and stiffly, he straightened, looking all around.

The countess is right. He has aged, Belle thought. *From grief. From loneliness and worry.*

"Papa, over here!" she called out.

Maurice turned. His eyes found hers, but they didn't

widen with surprise or delight. They were merely polite, the look in them inquiring. As if he didn't recognize her.

Had she changed so much in the time they'd been apart? *Perhaps it's the fine gown, the fancy bonnet,* she thought frantically. *Nevermore* had once again transformed her clothing, though the crystal heart the Beast had given her still hung from her neck.

"Papa, it's *me* . . . Belle," she cried, tearing her fancy hat off.

Maurice blinked at her. "Belle?" he said softly. "Can it be?"

"Papa. Oh, *Papa,*" she cried, her voice catching.

Her father's eyes filled with joy. His lips curved into a smile.

"*Belle,*" he said, his voice breaking. "My child, my darling, darling child. It's *you.*"

CHAPTER FORTY-ONE

FORGETTING THAT SHE WAS at the countess's estate, with beautiful strangers all around her, Belle ran to her father and threw herself, sobbing, into his arms.

Maurice held her tightly, stroking her hair, soothing her with soft words, just as he had when she was tiny.

"Shh, Belle, shh. It's all right. Come, child, let me look at you," he said, holding her at arm's length. "I thought I would never see you again. *Never*. And here you are . . . standing right in front of me!"

His happiness made Belle happy. The hitching in her chest subsided. She pulled her handkerchief from her pocket and wiped her tears away. He *was* real.

"I've missed you so much, my beautiful girl. How it gladdens my heart to see you," Maurice continued, still holding on to her. "How did you get here? Did you escape from that wicked beast?"

Belle realized that the last time her father had seen her, she'd been inside a prison cell at the Beast's castle—the same one he'd been in until she'd taken his place.

"I wasn't in that cell very long," she explained. "Lumiere, the Beast's footman, let me out. I live in the castle now, Papa, and am treated well. I have friends there—"

Maurice's face darkened. "Friends?" he said. "At that godforsaken place? You have jailers, Belle. You have dangerous objects—"

Dangerous? Belle thought. Mrs. Potts? Plumette?

"I know they may not have seemed this way to you, but they're very nice, Papa!" she interjected. "In fact, I've grown extremely fond of a little teacup named Chip, and—"

But her father wasn't listening. "You have a creature that dresses like a man but behaves like an animal, one who lashes out at everything and everyone," he continued. "Do not believe for a second that he, or anyone associated with him, is your friend!"

Belle wondered at her father's sharp words. He had always been an open-minded man, always willing to hear other points of view even when they were contrary to his own.

"The Beast was fearsome at first, yes," she said. "But the more time I spend with him, the more he surprises me. I think he may even be genuinely kind."

Maurice dismissed her words. "He has frightened the wits out of you, Belle. That much is plain to see," he said. "You speak well of him from fear, my child—thinking that if you do not, it will go all the worse for you."

Belle, who only moments ago had been angry at the Beast for imprisoning first her father and then herself, now felt herself bound to defend him. The dizzying shift of emotion confused her.

Belle's head said that to do such a thing was madness; that it made no sense. But her heart saw more than her head did, and it spoke with a deeper logic.

"Papa, do you remember Androcles?"

"Yes, of course. Our . . . uh, our neighbor."

"Our *neighbor*?" Belle repeated, blinking at him.

The countess was right. He *had* aged. The shock of finding himself imprisoned in the Beast's castle, and then losing his only child, had addled him.

"No, Papa," she said gently. "Androcles from *Aesop's Fables*! You used to read it to me every night."

"Of course, of course," Maurice quickly said.

CHAPTER FORTY-ONE

"The Beast is like the lion, with a thorn lodged deeply in him," Belle said.

Maurice's bushy eyebrows shot up. "You've seen this thorn, then?"

"The thorn is in his *heart*, Papa. Something terrible has befallen him."

But Maurice was in not in a charitable frame of mind. "Why are we spending our time talking about the Beast? I don't care about him. All I care about is you," he said. "How did you get here, Belle? When did you meet the countess?"

Belle explained how she'd found her way to *Nevermore.*

"An enchanted book, you say?" Maurice asked, when she'd finished.

"Yes. The countess put it where I would find it. She discovered what happened to us, Papa. She wants to help us. Because she knew my mother and was fond of her. She told me so."

Maurice's truculent expression melted. His eyes became soft and wistful, as they always did at the mention of his wife.

"That sounds like the countess. She's a kind soul. She always has been," Maurice said. "Here, at *her* home, I can pick a rose for my daughter without getting myself locked up," he said, as he turned and plucked a white bloom for Belle.

Belle took the rose from him. As she did, though, she saw a dark streak on its petals.

233

"Papa, you're bleeding!" she exclaimed, taking his hand. "You must've pricked yourself on a thorn."

"It's nothing," Maurice said, but droplets of blood, so dark they looked almost black, were falling onto the ground.

Belle was still clutching her handkerchief. "Here," she said. "This will stop it."

As she wrapped the cloth around his thumb and knotted it, she noticed that his hands were icy. "You're so cold!" she said, trying to chafe some warmth into them.

His cold hands, his stiff movements, the fact that he'd forgotten who Androcles was—these things troubled Belle greatly.

"Are you looking after yourself, Papa?" she asked fretfully. "Are you taking your cod-liver oil? You're not leaving the windows open at night, are you? You know how drafty the house gets. . . ."

"I'm fine, Belle," he said reassuringly. "It's *you* I'm worried about. I don't want you to go back to the Beast's castle. There must be some way to keep you here."

"Mademoiselle Belle!" said a voice. "Is that you?"

It was Henri. He was striding toward them with a spring in his step and a smile on his handsome face.

CHAPTER FORTY-TWO

"WHAT A PLEASURE IT IS to see you again!" Henri exclaimed, bowing to Belle.

"Likewise," said Belle, happy to see him. "Henri, I'd like you to meet my father, Maurice. Papa, this is my friend, Henri, duc des Choses-Passées."

"I'm honored to meet you, sir," Henri said, bowing again.

"The honor, young man, is all mine," replied Maurice.

"The countess speaks so highly of your work," Henri continued. "Indeed, she takes every opportunity to show it to me. She's trying to make me jealous, and she's succeeding. I hope that I, too, may acquire one of your music boxes."

Belle saw that there was a smile on her father's face now.

He was glowing from the compliment. She silently thanked Henri for it.

"Maurice! I see you've met the duc des Choses-Passées!" trilled the countess as she walked over to them.

Maurice pulled himself up to his full height as the countess approached. "I have! What a delightful fellow!" he said.

"You've made a mistake inviting me here today, Madame Comtesse," Henri said mischievously. "I've already told Monsieur Maurice that the next music box he makes is *mine*."

"Ungrateful wretch!" scolded the countess, swatting Henri with her fan. "Come," she said, taking Maurice's arm. "Let's walk back to the gazebo. Mouchard will bring us refreshments. And Maurice, I will do my best to change your mind about who should buy your next music box." She cupped her hand to her mouth and loudly whispered, "I'll pay twice what you're asking!"

"Not fair!" Henri protested.

"Dear boy, all's fair in love, war, and the acquisition of music boxes," said the countess with a wink.

Henri smiled. He offered Belle his arm. "One thing you must learn about our dear countess," he said. "She really *hates* to lose."

CHAPTER FORTY-THREE

"MY WORD, BUT IT'S WARM TODAY," Maurice said, fanning himself.

"Have another drink of your lemonade, Papa," Belle said, refreshing his glass from a pitcher on the table. Then she fluffed the pillow behind his back. She hadn't been able to stop fussing over him—asking him constantly if he was comfortable enough, cool enough, if he was thirsty or hungry.

"You're too good to me, Belle," he said now, reaching for her hand.

"Nonsense, Papa."

They were sitting in the countess's shady gazebo, whiling away the hours. It was already past noon. Maurice had his sketch pad on his lap. The countess was fanning herself. Henri was reading aloud from a book of Shakespearean sonnets.

" 'Love is not love
Which alters when it alteration finds,
Or bends with the remover to remove:
O, no! it is an ever-fixed mark,
That looks on tempests, and is never shaken;
It is the star to every wandering bark,
Whose worth's unknown, although his height be taken.
Love's not Time's fool, though rosy lips and cheeks
Within his bending sickle's compass come;
Love alters not with his brief hours and weeks,
But bears it out even to the edge of doom.' "

The gazebo was situated next to a burbling stream, at the edge of the countess's cherry orchard. Mouchard, alert for any stray beetles or spiders, was prowling around it, pumping insect spray over every flower, bush, and shrub.

"Mouchard! Leave off that and fetch some sandwiches," the countess ordered.

Henri snapped his book shut. "Capital idea, Madame

Comtesse," he said. "All that reading has made me hungry. Shall we have some cherries, too?"

"You're a dear, Monsieur Henri. But what will you put them in?"

"Take my hat," said Maurice, not bothering to look up from his sketch pad. He absentmindedly picked up the countess's, which was on a chair next to him, and held it out to Henri.

"My dear sir, the countess will string me up alive if I put cherries in *that*," Henri said, nodding at the black silk confection.

Maurice looked up. He peered at the object in his hand. "My word. Where did this come from? Where's *my* hat?"

"You're still *wearing* it, Papa," said Belle fondly.

She removed his broad-brimmed straw hat and kissed the top of his head. Maurice smiled and kept on sketching.

"Belle, do you fancy a stroll?" Henri asked.

"Thank you, Henri, but I think I'll stay here," Belle replied.

"Don't be silly, child. Go and stretch your legs. I'll be fine," Maurice said.

"Do, Belle," the countess quickly said. "Enjoy yourself. I'll keep an eye on him."

"If you're sure . . ." Belle said to her father.

Maurice said he was, and Belle and Henri set off for the cherry orchard. Henri was oddly quiet as they strolled. Belle noticed and asked him why.

"Ah, Belle. You know me too well. If I've been quiet, it's because I'm trying to figure out how to say what I have to say," he explained, giving her a vexed smile.

Belle glanced at him from under her hat brim. "What do you mean?"

"I . . . I've been called home. To my duchy in the north. There are problems on my estate. A blight's destroying my crops. I need to find a way to stop it, or there will be no harvest this year. And then my farmers, and their animals, will go hungry."

"Henri, that's terrible. I'm so sorry to hear it. When do you have to leave?" Belle asked.

"This afternoon," he replied.

Belle's face fell. "So soon?"

Henri nodded. He stopped, and Belle did, too. They were standing at the edge of the orchard.

"Belle . . ." He took her hand in his, glancing down. "May I ask something of you?"

"Anything, Henri."

He looked up at her, his eyes full of feeling. "Your friendship means a great deal to me. I've never met anyone as caring as you are. Anyone I can talk to so freely. Might I have a keepsake from you? Something to remind me of you while I'm gone?"

"Of course, Henri," Belle said.

She looked down at herself. Her plain blue dress had once again been transformed to a lovely gown when she had entered *Nevermore*; her boots had become silk shoes, and a pretty hat graced her head. But she could hardly give Henri a shoe or a hat.

"But I don't have anything to give you," she said, dismayed.

Henri's eyes fell on the delicate hollow under her throat and on the necklace she was wearing. "You have our hearts, Belle—mine and the countess's and everyone else's in *Nevermore*. Might I be so bold as to ask for yours?"

Belle hesitated. The necklace was a gift from the Beast. It had belonged to his mother, and Belle didn't want to give it away. Even though it was only glass, it was priceless, as were all things that had once been loved.

"I'll keep it safe and return it to you when I return to you," Henri pressed.

"I can't," Belle said. "It was a gift from . . . from a . . ."

What? Belle wondered. *What is the Beast to me? I wanted him to be my friend. At times, I thought he wanted me for a friend, too. But I was wrong.*

"Someone who means something to you?" Henri offered.

"Yes," Belle said, knowing she would have to be satisfied with that. Now and forevermore.

"I understand," said Henri. But his face fell at her reluctance. He quickly smiled, trying to cover his disappointment, but Belle couldn't bear his unhappiness.

"I wish I had something else," she said, thrusting her hands into her pockets.

She felt a lump in her right one and reached inside it. Her fingers curled around the small silver scissors the madwoman had given her. She'd forgotten all about them. She considered giving them to Henri, but decided scissors would be a strange keepsake.

Her other hand closed on coins—the ones she'd tried to give to Monsieur Truqué at the Palais-Royal.

"A sou?" she offered. "It's a bit odd, I know, but it was actually a keepsake for me—a memory of my home and my father."

"That would be perfect," said Henri, brightening. "It's so small, I can carry it with me wherever I go."

"Here you are," Belle said, handing him the coin.

CHAPTER FORTY-THREE

"Thank you, Belle. Thank you so much," said Henri.

He took the coin.

And put it in his pocket.

And that was when the cracks appeared.

Down both sides of his perfect, handsome, smiling face.

CHAPTER FORTY-FOUR

BELLE STARED IN SHOCK.

"Henri? What's wrong? Your—your face . . ." she stammered.

The cracks around his mouth had deepened into grooves.

Belle reached out to touch him. As she did, his jaw dropped open.

"Ha, ha, ha!" he laughed, his jaw clacking up and down. "Ha, ha, ha!"

Belle screamed and backed away. Henri walked toward her, his steps jerky and unnatural.

"My lady! Papa!" she shouted. "Come quick! There's something wrong with Henri!"

At the sound of Belle's cry, the countess rose from her chair and stepped down from the gazebo, her black skirts rustling.

Her guests stopped dead wherever they were—in the trees, by the stream, on the lawns.

A loud crash coming from the gazebo made Belle scream again. She turned around, terrified now. A fig tree in a terracotta pot had toppled over. Except, Belle now saw, it wasn't a fig tree at all. It was only a painted wooden cutout propped up by a stand.

Belle pressed her hands to her eyes. "What's happening?" she asked tearfully.

"Darling girl, what's wrong?"

Belle lowered her hands. It was the countess. Thank goodness. She clutched her arm.

"I don't know what's wrong. Look at Henri. Look at the others." Her voice was shaking. "We have to leave, my lady. Now. *Nevermore* . . . it's not what it seems. It's falling apart. We have to get my father and go back to the real world."

The countess patted Belle's hand. "I'm sorry, my dear, truly I am. But there is no way back. Not for you."

"What do you mean?" asked Belle, bewildered.

The countess smiled. "Why, you've eaten three things, haven't you?"

"I-I have?" Belle said, trying desperately to remember exactly what she'd eaten and what it might have to do with what was happening.

"The macaron at the ball . . ." the countess prompted.

"The tea cake at the Palais-Royal," Belle whispered.

"What was the third?" the countess said, tapping her chin. "Ah! I remember now! A pear!"

Panic gripped Belle. The countess was her friend, wasn't she? Then why was she trying to trap her?

"You've also left three things," the countess said. "When you take things and leave things in *Nevermore*, you become bound to it."

"But I didn't leave three things," Belle said adamantly.

Henri lurched forward. His painted face was as pale as a clown's. His teeth were bits of white porcelain. His beautiful jacket was garish and patched. Belle saw now that the charming, witty man whom she'd thought was her friend was nothing but a fairground puppet.

He held up the copper sou she'd given him. "Tsk, tsk, tsk," he said, wagging a wooden finger.

Belle felt sick.

Terror threatened to overwhelm her. She fought it down, refusing to give in to it. She knew she had to keep her head.

CHAPTER FORTY-FOUR

"That's one thing," she told the countess. "You said three things."

"True," said the countess. "This is another."

She lifted her arm and showed Belle the bracelet she was wearing. It was made from strands of hair—brown hair. The strands had been braided together, wound around the countess's wrist several times, and fastened with a gold clasp.

"I didn't give that to you," Belle said. "I've never even seen it before."

"Ah, but you have. It's your hair. It got snagged in my ring the night of the ball. Don't you remember?"

Belle felt her blood run cold. "That makes two things."

"Maurice?" said the countess.

Belle's father stepped down from the gazebo and joined them.

"Papa," Belle said, relief in her voice. He would know how to get out of here. He would save them both.

Maurice smiled at her. There was a little square of cloth tucked in his breast pocket. He pulled it out now and leaned forward to show it to her. Belle saw that it was stained and realized that it was the handkerchief she'd given him when he'd pricked his finger on a rose thorn.

"Number three," he said.

"Papa, I—I don't understand. Why?" Belle asked, her voice breaking. Had her own father betrayed her? The thought made her feel sick to her very soul.

But Maurice didn't answer her. He was still leaning forward. He hadn't moved. It seemed as if he were frozen. As Belle continue to plead with him, his hair suddenly slipped off his head and fell into the grass. She gasped.

The countess glared at him. "Mouchard!" she barked.

Mouchard hurried to her side, a brass key in his hands. It looked like the kind used to wind a mantel clock but much larger. He stuck the key into Maurice's back and turned it.

Maurice straightened, and Belle saw that what she had thought was her father wasn't at all.

"King Otto," she said, with a shock of recognition. "The automaton from the Palais-Royal!"

As she watched, the creature tucked the handkerchief back into its pocket. Then it picked up the wig and patted it back on its head.

"This . . . this *thing* looks nothing like my father," Belle said, aghast. "How could I have ever believed it was?"

"Appearances *can* be deceiving," the countess said smugly.

"Even more so if you enchant a marionette to look like a duke, or a vulture to resemble a butler, rather than conjuring them from scratch. Conserves magic, you see."

"This—this is *all* an enchantment . . . an illusion?" Belle stammered.

"Indeed. Like all good books," the countess said. "But you knew that, Belle."

"But it *seemed* so real."

"Because you wanted it to be. And now you're part of the story, too. *Nevermore* has pulled you in. In fact, I'd say you can't put it down." She nodded at Belle's hands.

Belle raised them. Words were printed on them in black, as if her skin was a page in a book. As she watched, more appeared.

"Make it stop," she pleaded. *"Please!"*

"It's too late. *Nevermore's* writing the ending, Belle. *Your* ending."

Belle's entire body went cold. "Why?" she asked, looking at the countess. "Why did you do this?"

"Because I made a wager, and I *hate* to lose," the countess replied.

Belle shook her head, stunned. "My life . . . it's a *game* to you?"

"I tried to give you a sporting chance, Belle. I dropped so many clues," the countess said. "The black dresses? The scythes on my coat of arms? Statues of Hades and Persephone? No? Ah, well. Humans are good at denial. Especially when it comes to me."

"What was the wager?"

"That death would win over love."

"Whom did you make the bet with?"

"Love herself. Be glad you didn't tangle with *her*, my dear. She's merciless. An utter savage."

"More so than you?" asked Belle bitterly.

The countess tilted her head. She lifted the glass heart the Beast had given Belle, smiled, and let it drop again.

"You understand so little, child," she said. "To love, to *truly* love another—that is not for the faint of heart. Why, I've seen a husband mop the brow of his plague-ridden wife, heedless of his own safety. I've seen a murderer's mother weep at the gallows, and a starving boy give his last crust of bread to his sister. Love is so strong, so ferocious, that she frightens even me. *Me*, Belle. A woman who strolls through battlefields and sick houses. Who takes tea with executioners."

Anger and defiance rose up in Belle, pushing her fear down. She thought of her father. Of Chip, Lumiere, Mrs. Potts. And the Beast.

"Love can still win," she declared defiantly. "It *will* win. I'm going to get out of here."

"Mmm, no. I don't think so," the countess said regretfully. "But I wouldn't fret about it too much. It won't take long. A day or two at most."

"I'll leave *Nevermore*. I'll find a way," Belle vowed.

"You know, I did worry, just for a bit, that I might actually lose this little game," the countess admitted. "After all, you're a formidable player. You gave up your freedom so that your father might regain his. Which was very commendable. Courageous, even. But then again, it's easy to love those who've done right by us, don't you think? A bit harder to love those who've done us wrong."

At that moment, a fearsome vulture with a cruel beak and black feathers swooped down. He landed on the gazebo's railing, shook his wings, and squawked.

"Yes, Mouchard. I'm *coming*," the countess said.

She dipped her head to Belle. "Goodbye, my dear. I've enjoyed this game, but my work awaits me. I must get back to my château and pack. I leave in the morning. There are wars to attend. Pestilence, famine, the usual." She smiled coquettishly. "I am much in demand."

Then she turned away and walked toward the orchard, Mouchard circling above her.

She looked back once. "Don't be too angry with me," she said. "After all, I gave you what you wanted—a way out of the Beast's castle. You don't have to go back. And you didn't break your promise. I did it for you. I am the breaker of *all* promises, Belle. The ender of all vows."

And then the gloom that hung between the trees, even on this bright summer day, closed around her.

CHAPTER FORTY-FIVE

BELLE'S CHEST STARTED TO HITCH. Her breath was coming in short little gasps. The fear was back, squeezing her lungs so hard she couldn't get any air.

I'm going to die here, she thought. *My father, the Beast, Lumiere, and all the others . . . they'll never even know what happened to me.*

You'll definitely die here if you don't stop acting like a ninny, said a voice in her head. *Breathe,* the voice soothed. *In and out. Yes. Just like that.*

Belle focused on her breathing until it had slowed.

Very good. You've got it. Now think, Belle. Think hard.

"I got myself into *Nevermore.* I can get myself out," Belle said aloud. "But how?"

253

The way you got in, perhaps?

"Yes! Through the portal!" Belle shouted.

That meant getting herself back to the château, and this time there would be no carriage to take her. She'd have to walk, and it would be a long one, but she could manage; the beautiful gown she'd been wearing had turned back into her serviceable blue cotton dress, and the delicate silk shoes into her sturdy brown boots.

Having a plan calmed Belle and gave her courage. She looked around, trying to locate the graveled drive that led to the road.

She had been in such a state of shock that she hadn't registered her surroundings. The gazebo, she now saw, was actually a ramshackle chicken coop. The summer house was an abandoned ruin. Broken shutters hung crookedly from the windows. Ivy covered its walls and balconies. Its terraces were cracked and overgrown by weeds.

The things that had been the countess's guests—marionettes, dolls, and mannequins—wandered aimlessly. Some got caught in bushes and thrashed helplessly. One toppled into the stream. Another walked into a tree limb and knocked its head off. The head lay on the ground, eyes shifting from side to side, mouth a red O, while the body stumbled on.

Beyond the stream, in the distance, a line of twisted, broken tree trunks poked up like gnarled, blackened fingers along the far edge of the grounds.

Something about them looked familiar to Belle. She bit her lip, trying to remember, and then the answer came to her.

"They were the chestnut trees I saw from the carriage's window, the ones lining the drive. That's the way out!" Belle said excitedly.

She set off walking toward the trees, then broke into a run. But as soon as she did, the marionettes, dolls, and mannequins all stopped wandering. Their heads swiveled. Their painted eyes found Belle. Clattering and clanking, they shambled toward her, cutting her off from the drive.

Belle tried to skirt around them, but there were too many. They'd surrounded her. Bit by bit, they pushed her back to the summer house.

"Let me go! Get out of my way!" she shouted angrily, shoving one to the ground. She pushed another away. And then another.

And then, from their midst, Henri stepped forward.

His eyes, once so warm and full of life, had become cold, hard glass.

"Henri, please . . . let me pass," she said.

Henri's head moved from side to side. His eyelids

dropped, then snapped up again. Undeterred, Belle took a step toward him.

His arm shot out as if raised by invisible strings. Belle saw that he was holding a sword. The blade looked like wood that had been painted silver, but she couldn't be sure.

"Henri," she said, "Let. Me. Go."

Henri lunged. The tip of his sword stopped only inches from Belle's chest.

With a cry, she turned and ran inside the summer house.

As she crossed its threshold, the heavy doors slammed shut behind her with an ominous, deafening boom.

CHAPTER FORTY-SIX

"Αἱ περιστάσεις εἰσὶν αἱ τοὺς ἄνδρας δεικνύουσαι . . ." the Beast read aloud, carefully examining the ancient piece of parchment.

"Difficulties are things . . ." he slowly translated. Then he dipped his quill into the pot of ink on his desk and wrote the words down on a fresh piece of foolscap—the oversized, none-too-fine writing paper he used for his transcriptions.

"Difficulties are things . . ." he began again. "Ah! I have it. Difficulties are things that show people what they are!"

"He *must* be told!" trumpeted a voice.

It startled the Beast so that he dropped his quill, causing the nib to leave blots all over the foolscap.

"Quite true. And you're just the one to tell him."

"*Me*? Why not you?"

The Beast's gaze moved from the parchment to the open door of his study. Three shadows had fallen across the floor outside it.

"He *said* he wasn't to be interrupted!"

"But this is important!"

"That's quite right. He would want to know."

"So tell him!"

"You!"

"No, you!"

"No, *you*!"

The Beast squeezed his eyes shut. He rubbed his temples. The philosopher Epictetus was not easy to translate in perfect peace and quiet, never mind when a noisy teapot, a loud candelabrum, and a blustering clock were all gathered outside your door.

"Shh! The master's hard at work!" That was Cogsworth, speaking so loudly he might have been ordering twenty thousand cavalry into battle. "We must *not* disturb him!"

"It's a bit late for that," the Beast said, opening his eyes. "Do come in, Cogsworth. Mrs. Potts. Lumiere."

The three servants trooped inside, all casting baleful looks at each other.

"What is the matter?" asked the Beast, blotting his paper.

"We don't know," said Mrs. Potts.

The Beast's eyebrows shot up. "You don't know?"

"It's Belle," said Lumiere. "She's in the library. . . ."

"Belle is always in the library," said the Beast. "Why is that suddenly a cause for concern?"

"Because it appears that perhaps she is not," Cogsworth replied.

And then all three started talking at once.

"We don't know that," said Lumiere.

"We don't *not* know it, either!" said Cogsworth.

"But there were toasted cheese sandwiches!" said Mrs. Potts, inexplicably.

The Beast held up his paws. "One of you, please. Just one. Speak slowly, calmly, and above all, *rationally*."

Mrs. Potts took a deep breath. "We haven't seen her since breakfast, master, and it's six o'clock now," she said. "She didn't come downstairs at noon to dine as she usually does."

"Neither did I. Perhaps she is absorbed in her reading, as I am. Or *was*."

"It's most unlike her. She always comes down for the midday meal. Especially when Cuisinier makes toasted cheese sandwiches," Mrs. Potts explained. "When she didn't appear,

I decided to take some sandwiches up to her. But when I got to the library, she wouldn't answer the door no matter how loudly I called to her."

"Perhaps she didn't hear you. Perhaps you could try bringing the tray in to her."

"But that's just it, master. I *did* try opening the door. But I couldn't, because it's locked."

"Why?" the Beast asked, puzzled. "The doors to the library are never locked anymore."

"I don't know, master. That's why we've come. We're worried. Belle hasn't been herself lately."

The Beast's puzzlement turned to concern.

"It's all that Shakespeare," Cogsworth said darkly. "It's made her swoon. I'll wager she's lying unconscious on the floor, a copy of *Romeo and Juliet* nearby."

Mrs. Potts's worry lines deepened.

"I've also heard of certain persons being deathly allergic to the inks used for printing," said Cogsworth. "She may be gasping her last at this very moment."

Mrs. Potts paled.

"Not helpful, Cogsworth, old boy," said Lumiere, nodding at the fretful teapot.

But Cogsworth didn't hear him. "Then again, it's quite

possible that a bookcase has fallen over and squashed her flat," he said.

At which Mrs. Potts promptly started to sob.

"*Something* has happened! Something terrible! I'm sure of it!" she wailed. "Belle *never* turns down a toasted cheese sandwich."

"So much for Epictetus," the Beast sighed.

He was quite certain his servants were overreacting. He was also sure that no further work would be accomplished by anyone in the castle until Mrs. Potts, Lumiere, and Cogsworth had all laid eyes on Belle.

"She's very likely curled up in a comfortable chair by the fire, asleep with a book in her lap," said the Beast. "If there's one place in the castle we don't have to worry about Belle, it's the library." He stepped out from behind his desk. "Come along," he ordered, striding out of his study.

A few minutes later, the Beast and his servants were standing in front of the library's doors. Chip, Froufrou, and Plumette, having heard their agitated voices, had joined them.

The Beast tried the door handle. It was, indeed, locked.

"Belle?" he called out, knocking on the door.

Belle made no response.

The Beast's hackles rose. What if his servants were right

after all? Belle had looked so pale and listless at breakfast. What if she'd become ill?

"Belle?" he bellowed, hammering on the door. "Belle, are you all right?"

But he got no answer.

No answer at all.

CHAPTER FORTY-SEVEN

ON THE SECOND FLOOR of the abandoned summer house, in a crumbling room, Belle sat on a half-rotted window seat, hugging her knees.

She was safe from the marionettes, dolls, and automatons up there. The creatures had managed to get the summer house's doors open, but they'd had difficulty with the staircase. They couldn't get the stepping motion right. Some had made it halfway up only to lose their balance and pitch over the banister. Others had tumbled noisily down the steps, collapsing in a heap at the bottom.

They hadn't given up, though. At the sound of a particularly noisy crash, Belle lifted her head and glanced nervously at the door. She'd defiantly told the countess that she was going to get out of *Nevermore*, but how? She couldn't even get out of the summer house.

Despondent, she looked out the broken window.

Nevermore was fading.

The illusion the countess had spun was dissipating. The once lush-looking hills and dales of her estate were nothing more than a painted backdrop; the stream, a dry ditch.

Belle herself was fading.

The vivid blue of her dress now looked dull. Her brown boots looked colorless.

One thing was growing stronger and more vivid, though—the black print on her skin. It was no longer only on her hands, but was creeping up her forearms. The words of *Nevermore* were multiplying rapidly as they finished her story.

"The countess was right. I'm going to die here," she whispered.

A fly flew into the room and circled around Belle. Its buzzing drove her mad. She swatted at it, then abruptly stopped.

A bit of light came back into her eyes. She sat up straighter. The buzzing insect had given her an idea.

"Lucanos?" she said, in an uncertain voice.

The beetle had tried to help her before. Twice. She hadn't

listened to him either time, but if he gave her a third chance, she would.

"Lucanos! Are you there?" she called out, loudly this time. But the beetle didn't answer.

"I'm sorry, Lucanos! I should have followed your advice. I want to get out of here. I don't want Death to win. Can you help me? *Please?*"

Belle looked out of the window as she called to the beetle, craning her neck this way and that way, but she saw no sign of him.

"It's no use," she said dejectedly.

But then she *heard* something—a buzzing. It got louder and louder, and a few seconds later, a giant stag beetle flew in through the broken window and landed next to her.

"Lucanos!" she said joyfully.

"Indeed," the beetle replied, brushing dust off his wings.

He folded them neatly, and as he did, Aranae crawled over the sill. Both creatures looked around the room.

"Well, this is a fine mess, I must say," Lucanos declared.

Aranae chittered questioningly, pointing to Belle.

Lucanos nodded. "Yes, yes, Aranae. I'm quite certain," he said impatiently. "She's the girl who sees with her heart."

Aranae rolled all eight of her eyes. She chittered again, in a scolding tone this time. When she finished, she crossed two of her legs and gave Belle a dirty look.

Belle shrank under her disapproving glare. "What did she say?" she asked timidly.

"She said your heart needs glasses."

"I made a mistake, Lucanos. A terrible one."

"That, my dear, is an understatement."

"I didn't look past the surface. *Nevermore* was so beautiful and exciting, and the countess and Henri were so friendly and said all the things I wanted to hear. And I so badly wanted to see my father. I would have believed *anyone* who offered me that chance."

Tears welled. Belle tried to blink them away.

"What have I done?" she said. "I wanted to escape. From the Beast's castle. From my life. Now all I want is to go home, but I don't even know where home is anymore." Belle's tears spilled over. "Even if I *could* get out of this place, I wouldn't know where to go," she sobbed. "Where is it, Lucanos? Where *is* my home?"

The beetle sighed. He touched the tip of one leg to the place over Belle's heart. "It's here, foolish girl," he said. "Home is all the people, all the places, and all the things that you love. You carry it wherever you go. Don't you know that?"

Belle thought about Lucanos's words. She closed her eyes,

and an image of her father came to her. She thought of his beautiful music boxes, and of books. Of petting Philippe's soft nose. Of roses. And of other things, now, too. Dawn breaking over a winter landscape. The sound of Chip's laughter. Lumiere teasing Cogsworth. Mrs. Potts humming. Skating with the Beast on a frozen lake.

"I do now," she said, opening her eyes.

"We all make mistakes," Lucanos said. "The danger lies in letting those mistakes make us."

"Make us what?" asked Belle.

"Make us believe we can't put things right. Make us think there's no hope. Make us give up," the beetle said, giving Belle a very direct look.

Belle understood what he was telling her. She wiped her face on her skirt and said, "I want to get out of here, Lucanos. Can you help me?"

"Getting out of *Nevermore* is easier said than done, I'm afraid."

"Why? What *is* this place, exactly? One big illusion?"

"*Nevermore* is much more than an illusion, child. It is very real."

"But the countess said—"

"She lied. Most of the things in it—the marionettes, the ruins, the grounds—were enchanted to deceive you, but

267

Nevermore itself is a realm. Death's realm. It's a place of unbecoming. Of rot, decay, and ruin."

A shiver ran through Belle, but she shook it off, determined to be brave. To take charge.

Lucanos noticed. "That's more like it," he said. "Now, let's see if we can get you out of here. We've got to be bold, quick, and cunning, because our adversary is all those things and more."

"Thank you for coming, Lucanos. You, too, Aranae," Belle said.

"Thank us when you get out of here," Lucanos said wryly.

Then the three huddled together and started to make a plan.

CHAPTER FORTY-EIGHT

"BELLE? BELLE! ARE YOU IN THERE? Are you all right?" the Beast called out. He was shouting now.

But still, there was no answer.

"I'm very worried, master," said Mrs. Potts.

"So am I," the Beast said grimly.

Mrs. Potts had been right when she'd said that Belle hadn't been herself lately, but he knew Belle would never do this— lock herself in the library and leave them all to wonder and worry. She was far too considerate to do something like that.

"Stand clear, everyone," he said, taking a step back from the doors.

The enchanted objects quickly moved away. As they did,

the Beast launched himself at the right-hand door, ramming it with his shoulder. It shuddered under the impact of his powerful body, but held.

He did it again, ignoring the pain that shot through his arm, but again the door held.

Desperate, he backed up one last time. Then, with an ear-splitting roar, he drove his shoulder against the unyielding door. Finally it gave way.

Growling, he pushed his way in through the splintered wood.

Something was not right. The Beast felt it in his bones.

He raced through the library, calling Belle's name, hoping he was not too late.

CHAPTER FORTY-NINE

LUCANOS SAT UPRIGHT on the windowsill, two of his spiny black legs crossed, two more folded across his chest. He stroked his chin with his fifth leg, and the sixth waved in the air as he spoke.

"The food you've eaten helps bind you to *Nevermore*," he said. "You swallowed both of those sweets, and that pear, which I'm sorry to say, was really a pomegranate."

"The food of the dead," Belle said, her hopes of escape faltering. "In the Greek myth, Persephone ate pomegranate seeds and had to return to the underworld. I'm doomed, Lucanos."

"We're all doomed," Lucanos said matter-of-factly. "We're all going to find ourselves here one day. But that day is *not* today. Not if I can help it."

Aranae chittered. Lucanos nodded at her.

"What did she say?" Belle asked anxiously.

"She said there's nothing we can do about the food. So stop talking about it," he replied.

Belle feverishly racked her brain for another angle. "What about the three things I gave away?" she asked. "What if I got them back? Would it weaken the countess's spell?"

"Interesting question," said Lucanos. "Quite possibly."

"If it *did* weaken the spell, maybe I could slip back through the enchanted book."

"But that means getting the handkerchief from King Otto, the coin from Henri, and the bracelet from the countess herself," Lucanos said direly.

"Yes, it does."

"So you're saying that we need to outfox Death," Lucanos said.

Belle nodded.

"*Death*, Belle."

"It's not the surest of plans, admittedly," said Belle. "But I don't have a better one."

"All right, then," the beetle said, eyeing the writing on Belle's hands, which was now creeping up her arms. "No more dillydallying. Time is not on our side. Let's go pay court to the king."

CHAPTER FIFTY

WARILY, BELLE MADE HER WAY down the summer house's staircase with Lucanos and Aranae at her side.

They passed a clockwork man slumped on the stairs. Its staring eyes were empty, its body lifeless, but its feet were still trying to climb the steps.

"They're running down," Lucanos whispered. "That's good. It means the countess's enchantment is weakening. If you can get the objects back, you should be able to break out of it."

As the three reached the bottom of the staircase, they had to sidestep a pile of broken, twitching figures—the marionettes and mannequins who'd pursued Belle and tumbled down the stairs. Heads were smashed, limbs were twisted.

Neither King Otto nor Henri was among them.

"They've got to be here somewhere," Belle said.

The three continued. As they moved through the ruined rooms, they heard strange, dissonant music playing. It sounded faraway, as if coming from another part of the summer house. They saw puppets slumped in corners and a doll collapsed on a tattered chaise, sawdust spilling from its seams. On either side of a marble mantel, the countess's elegant greyhounds sat, now motionless stone statues.

Everywhere Belle looked, surfaces revealed what they'd been concealing. Rot bloomed across mirrors. Holes gaped in the ceiling where plaster had fallen. Mildew crept over curtains and rugs. The crystal chandeliers were gray with dust. Tarnish blackened the candelabra.

Fury roiled inside Belle. The countess had lied to her. Manipulated her. Controlled her. It wasn't fair. If the countess was Death, then Death was a cheat.

As they passed the doorway of the countess's study, Belle paused. Her eyes swept over the bookcases. The books they contained were tattered and mildewed. Rusted gears, springs, and dials lay on the shelves next to them. Belle remembered being in this room with the countess and the professor. She remembered looking at all the pieces of rusted junk and believing they were her father's music boxes. The memory sickened her now.

Her gaze roved over the rest of the study. She saw broken furniture and a crumbling mantel, and then she saw something that made her blood run cold. She motioned to Lucanos and Aranae, then pointed into the room.

King Otto was standing at the back of it, next to an open window, perfectly still. The automaton's back was toward them. Belle could see the brass key protruding from it. One hand was raised above its head; a butterfly had lighted on it and was slowly beating its yellow wings.

"It looks like it's wound down," Lucanos whispered. "What a stroke of luck!"

Carefully the three proceeded toward it, alert for the slightest movement. As they got closer, Belle could see that her handkerchief was still tucked into its breast pocket. Her heart was knocking against her ribs. Just a few more steps, and the handkerchief would be hers again.

"Grab it. Be quick," Lucanos urged her. "We have no time to waste."

Belle nodded. She stretched out her hand. But just as her fingers were about to close on it, the butterfly darted off.

And Otto angrily whirled around.

CHAPTER FIFTY-ONE

"YOU SCARED IT!" the automaton said accusingly, taking a threatening step toward Belle. "It was just telling me what it feels like to fly!"

"I-I'm sorry," Belle stammered. "I didn't mean to."

"Now I'll *never* know!" the creature shouted, stamping its foot.

Belle backed away, frightened. She thought it might chase her. Instead, it took a few slow, stiff steps, then burst into tears. Droplets of black oil leaked from its eyes and ran down its cheeks. It wiped them away with Belle's handkerchief.

Belle was so surprised, she could only stand there gaping.

Lucanos flew to her shoulder. "Stay perfectly still. Speak calmly. Don't make it mad," he said.

"I have *ears*, you know! And I'm not an *it*. My name is O-O-Otto," the creature said between sobs.

Belle, moved by the automaton's tears, forgot about her fear. She took a hesitant step toward him.

"You don't have to be scared. I couldn't chase you if I wanted to," Otto said, snuffling. "It's hard to move. My joints are stiff. Now that the countess has what she wants—*you*—she's no longer keeping the illusions up. Everything's collapsing. The things that took a lot of effort to animate, like me, will last a bit longer, but the orchards, the flowers—they're already going."

As he spoke, a new crack opened up in a wall. Seeing it, Otto launched into a fresh volley of weeping.

"Otto, why are you crying?" Belle asked, putting a gentle hand on his shoulder.

"Because I *liked* being alive!" he howled, burying his face in the handkerchief.

"We don't have *time* for this, Belle," Lucanos cautioned.

But Belle didn't hear him. She was listening to Otto. He'd wiped his face and stuffed the handkerchief into his breast pocket.

"I was made in Paris. The countess saw me perform there

and bought me from my maker. I was always so jealous of the humans who came to watch me," he explained. "Just now, when I was almost human, I was nearly able to understand what you feel. Why you laugh or cry. I almost felt the thing I've always most wanted to feel . . . love."

He paused and smiled, but the smile was bittersweet.

"I've seen how humans love each other," he continued. "It's amazing. Once, when my maker was loading me into his wagon after a show, I saw a father push his son out of the way of a runaway carriage. The father saved his boy, but he was killed." Otto shook his head, awed by the memory. "How powerful love must be, to make a creature do something like that."

"It is," Belle said, thinking of her father and how she'd taken his place in Beast's castle so he could go free.

"I wish I could know what that's like. I never will, though." His hand went to his pocket. He pulled Belle's handkerchief out and handed it to her.

Belle looked at it. What had seemed to her to be blood was really oil.

"It's the best I can do. It's something. I-I tried to love you, Belle. When I was pretending to be your father," Otto said. He touched her cheek gently with his papier-mâché hand. "I tried, but I couldn't. I think you need a heart for that—and I haven't got one."

"Oh, Otto," Belle said, hugging him tightly. As she rubbed his back, her gaze fell upon a window behind him, and the tattered red silk draperies that framed it.

She remembered the silver scissors in her pocket.

"Wait right here," she instructed Otto, releasing him.

In an instant she was at the window, ripping a silk panel down. She laid it on the floor, smoothed it flat, and started cutting.

Lucanos held a claw to his ear. "Time?" he said, as if she'd asked him how much they had. "Oh, don't worry about *that*. We have *buckets* of it! We only have to catch Death before she departs her château to wreak havoc on the world, so take all day, Belle, do."

It was hard going; the scissors were small and hadn't been made to cut fabric, but after a few minutes, Belle sat back on her heels and held up what she'd made—a tattered silk heart.

She put her scissors back in her pocket, then called to Aranae. "Can you help me?"

The spider huffed impatiently, but she took the heart in her fangs. Then she scuttled over to Otto and climbed up to his chest. Otto looked at Belle questioningly, but she just nodded at him, biting her lip and hoping.

Working quickly, Aranae placed the cloth heart over the spot on Otto's chest where his real heart would've been had he been human. Using her fangs, she punched holes through the heart, and using her claws and spider silk, she stitched it to Otto's jacket. When she finished, she patted the heart and jumped down.

Otto caught his breath. Color flooded his cheeks. He looked down at his heart wonderingly, then smiled at Belle.

"I *know* now! I know what it means to be alive! Love is its own magic. And it's strong. So strong!" He twirled around, arms spread wide. "I love you, Belle! I love you, spider! And you, too, beetle!"

Belle's heart swelled. She smiled back at Otto.

Lucanos tensed with frustration. "That's so great, Otto. I'm happy for you. Truly," he said. "But if we don't get the coin from Henri and then get out of here, Belle is going. To. *Die.*"

Otto, still twirling, said, "I'll help you! I love helping!"

Lucanos closed his eyes. He rubbed his forehead. "Otto," he said, "if you want to help us, stop spinning around and tell us where Henri is. Tell us how to get the coin from him. We've got to come up with a way, because I doubt very much we're going to win *him* over with a cutout heart."

CHAPTER FIFTY-TWO

"BELLE!" THE BEAST BELLOWED. *"BELLE!"*

He was standing in the middle of the library, his paws clenched.

He'd broken the door down and pushed his way into the library, certain he'd find her here. The others had followed him inside and fanned out through the room, calling for Belle.

But Belle had not answered.

"She's not here, master," Lumiere said as he rejoined the Beast. Cogsworth, Mrs. Potts, and Plumette followed him.

"We've looked *everywhere!*" Plumette said.

"She's left us," the Beast said, voicing everyone's deepest fear. "She's gone back to Villeneuve."

"But, master, the wolves . . ." Mrs. Potts said, distressed.

"Fetch my cloak," the Beast said grimly. "I'm going out to look for her."

"What if it's too late? What if the wolves—" Plumette said, her feathers trembling.

Mrs. Potts cut her off. "Don't say that! Don't even *think* it!"

The Beast held his paws up. "Wait a moment. This makes no sense. How could Belle have left? The library doors were locked from the inside."

"What about a window?" Cogsworth asked. "She might have jumped from one and used the snowdrifts to cushion her fall. I did the very same thing once, having been taken prisoner by the Prussians at the battle of Vellinghausen. . . ."

No one stuck around to hear Cogsworth's story; they all raced to the windows.

"She didn't jump out of this one. It's still locked!" Lumiere called out.

"Same here!" Mrs. Potts shouted.

"She would have left footprints in the snow, and there aren't any," said the Beast, perplexed. "Where *is* she? How could she have just disappeared?"

At that moment, they all heard a loud, frantic barking coming from the back of the library. A second later, Chip hurtled toward them, breathless. Froufrou was right behind him.

"This way!" Chip said, panting. *"Hurry!"*

"Chip, did you find her?" Mrs. Potts asked.

"No, but come with me! Hurry!" he begged. "I think I know where she went!"

CHAPTER FIFTY-THREE

"I LOVE YOU, BELLE," said Otto happily.

Belle turned around. She held a finger to her lips. "I love you, too, Otto. But could you be a little quieter?" she whispered.

Otto nodded energetically. "I love you, Aranae!" he whispered.

He clumsily ran to catch up with Lucanos, who was flying next to Belle. "I love you, too, little black beetle!"

"Good grief, man. Get hold of yourself!" Lucanos said, shuddering.

Otto clutched his chest. "That hurts my heart!" he said.

"Your heart—and all the rest of you—will hurt a lot more if Henri finds us before we find him!" Lucanos hissed.

Otto scowled.

"Also, can you not *clank*?" Lucanos asked irritably.

"I can't help it!" Otto retorted.

Belle turned around. "Shh!" she cautioned, glaring at them both.

They had left the study where they'd found Otto and were now looking for Henri.

"I'm sure he can't hear us. Who could hear *anything* over that horrible music?" said Otto.

Belle and her friends were approaching the conservatory, and the music they'd heard earlier was louder now, the notes harsher and more discordant.

"What if it's *Henri* who's making that horrible music?" asked Lucanos.

"There's only one way to find out," said Belle as they reached the conservatory. The room's huge double doors were open and folded back against the wall. She inched up to one and peered around it.

A marionette was seated at a harpsichord, playing. His movements were jerky, his shoulders sharp under his moth-eaten jacket.

Worried he might suddenly turn around and see her, Belle stepped back out of sight.

"Is it him?" Lucanos asked.

"It's him," Belle whispered, leaning against the door. A shudder ran through her. "How are we going to get the coin?"

"It's very simple," said Otto.

Lucanos rolled his eyes. "What do you suggest? That we hug him to death?"

"No, that we cut his strings. He's a marionette, isn't he? He must have strings," said Otto.

"Otto, that's brilliant!" Belle whispered. "If we cut his strings, he can't come after us."

Otto grinned.

Lucanos crawled to the doorway, then crawled back. "I don't see any strings," he said.

"That doesn't mean they're not there," Otto said. "When the countess enchanted him, she would've made them invisible. If we can just get to him, we can finish him off!"

"Yes," said the beetle. He cast a worried glance at the doors. "As long as . . ."

"As long as what?" Otto prompted.

"As long as *he* doesn't finish *us* off first."

CHAPTER FIFTY-FOUR

BELLE STOOD IN THE DOORWAY, her scissors in her hand.

Her heart was thumping so hard now, she was certain Henri would hear it.

Summoning all her courage, she slid one foot in front of her, then the other. Step by step, she crossed the room. Lucanos and Aranae crept noiselessly behind her. Otto stayed by the doors in case he clanked.

Henri continued to play his jangling, macabre piece, and Belle prayed that he would be too absorbed in the music to sense her presence. As she drew closer, she saw that something was vibrating above him.

His strings! she thought. *Otto was right!*

The countess's magic was releasing its grip, even on Henri. Belle saw that the strings ran from his head, jaw, shoulders, and wrists. More were attached to his legs. Her eyes followed them up. They seemed to disappear into the air.

Which do I cut first? she wondered. *The strings controlling his hands, so he can't grab me? Or his feet, so he can't run after me?*

Belle remembered the malicious expression on Henri's face after she'd given him her coin. She remembered how he'd forced her into the summer house. What if she couldn't cut the strings before he realized what she was doing? What if she couldn't cut them at all?

Belle's nerve almost failed her right then and there, but she willed herself to keep going.

Just a few snips, she told herself, *and you'll have the coin back.*

Slowly, quietly, she closed the distance between herself and Henri. Ten yards became eight, then three. And then she was right behind him, close enough to see the badly sewn patches on his jacket, the wig made out of a horse's tail, and the joints of his wooden hands.

Now, Belle, she told herself. *Be quick. Be brave.*

She raised the scissors, opening their blades wide.

And that was when Henri's head spun suddenly, sickeningly, around.

CHAPTER FIFTY-FIVE

HENRI'S GLASS EYES GLINTED MADLY, his lips twisted into a cruel smile.

"Do you like this piece, Belle?" he asked her. "I composed it myself. I call it 'Prelude to a Death.'"

Then he shot to his feet and knocked the scissors from Belle's hand. They clattered to the floor.

"No!" Belle cried. She lunged for them, but Henri grabbed her wrist and jerked her back.

"Let me go!" she shouted, trying to break free.

But he only tightened his grip, squeezing her wrist so cruelly that she sank to her knees. "What's the matter? Don't you like this story anymore?" he asked.

Otto, clutching his cutout heart, ran into the room.

"Hang on, Belle! I'm coming! I'll save you!" he shouted, heading for the scissors.

But before he could reach them, he tripped, fell, and collapsed in a heap. One of his ears fell off. His left leg bent backward at the knee.

"Otto? Is that you?" Henri asked contemptuously. "What are you doing here?"

"Helping my friend," Otto said, struggling to sit up.

"You're an automaton, you fool. You have no friends."

"I *do*," Otto stubbornly insisted, pointing to his fabric heart. "Belle gave me this. She loves me."

Henri laughed, showing his porcelain teeth. "You're nothing but a clattering pile of junk! You don't even know what love is."

"I *didn't* know what love was," Otto admitted earnestly, "until Belle loved me."

"She only loved you when she thought you were her father," Henri said.

"Well, now she loves the real me. *Otto*."

Henri snorted. "A lot of good it does you. You're so broken, you can't even stand up!" He shook his head. "Of all the idiotic emotions humans possess, love's the most idiotic. Don't you agree, Belle?"

Belle looked at Otto, who had struggled, and failed, to

straighten his twisted leg and was now pulling himself across the floor, inch by inch, still trying to get to the scissors. Otto, who rattled and stumbled and dripped and fell apart, but who didn't give up.

She thought of Mrs. Potts making her tea and bringing her toasted cheese sandwiches. And Lumiere, Cogsworth, and Plumette helping her clean the library. And Chip sprinkling breadcrumbs in the snow with her.

Because they love me. Because they're my friends, she thought.

She thought of the Beast skating with her, even though he was bad at it, because it made her happy. She remembered him giving her the library because she loved to read. She remembered him fighting off a pack of wolves for her.

Maybe I've been wrong about him, she thought. *Maybe he is a friend. Not the easiest one I ever had, but still . . . a friend.*

She thought of Pere Robert, Agathe, and her father.

And then she got to her feet. "No, Henri, I *don't* agree," she said. "Love isn't idiotic. It's hard and messy, confusing and wonderful. But to love and be loved . . . that's all that matters. Can't you see that?"

"Mmm, *no.* I'm afraid not," Henri said, feigning regret.

"Let me go, Henri. *Please,*" Belle begged.

And then, miraculously, Henri did.

CHAPTER FIFTY-SIX

THE MARIONETTE'S WOODEN HANDS released Belle and dropped to his sides. As they did, the cut ends of two strings slipped through the air with a hiss and landed on the floor.

"Thank you, Henri," Belle said, relief coursing through her.

"What? *No!* Don't *thank* me! I didn't mean to do it! What's happening?" Henri bellowed.

He jerked his shoulders, trying to raise his arms, but he couldn't. He looked up. Belle did, too. Lucanos, clinging to one of Henri's strings high above them, saluted.

"We climbed up here while you three were chatting about feelings," the beetle said. "Aranae bit through the string that works Henri's right hand. I bit through the one that works his left."

As the beetle finished speaking, there was a loud twang, and then Henri lurched alarmingly to his right.

"What the devil?" he yelled, looking around wildly.

Otto stood there, balancing uncertainly on his bent leg, scissors in hand. He'd severed the string to Henri's right shoulder.

"Stop it, Otto!" Henri shouted. "Squash the bugs and seize the girl! Now! Or you'll answer to *her!*"

There was another twang as Otto cut the string to Henri's left leg. Henri lurched forward, pivoting in a circle on his right leg.

"Come!" he shrieked. "All of you! Come to me, *now!*"

Belle glanced toward the door.

"Otto, cut the string to his jaw!" she shouted, but it was too late.

Henri had summoned the rest of the creatures in the summer house. They were shuffling toward the conservatory now with whatever magic was left in them.

Otto quickly snipped another string, then another. Henri's head lolled forward, then his torso. As Otto severed the string that was attached to his bottom, Henri clattered to the floor like a pile of firewood.

As he did, dozens of puppets and dolls began crowding through the doorway.

"There's no way out!" Otto cried.

Belle looked at the back of the room. Broken furniture lay strewn across it. Its far wall was lined by three pairs of French doors. "Get to the doors, Otto!" she yelled. "Hurry!"

She knelt down and quickly dug through the pockets of Henri's jacket. She found her coin, shoved it into her own pocket, and ran to the back of the room.

Aranae had climbed to safety high up on a wall. Lucanos, too. Belle grabbed the handle to a pair of doors and twisted, but it was locked. She tried the others, but they were locked, too.

"Destroy them!" Henri shouted. "All of them!"

Belle looked behind her. Otto was hobbling toward her as fast as he could, but it wasn't fast enough. The puppets and dolls were closing in on him. He was trying his hardest to get away from them, but his bad leg slowed him. Terror was etched on his face.

"No!" Belle screamed. "Get away from him!"

She dashed to him, slung one of his arms over her shoulder, and dragged him to the back of the room, where she leaned him against a desk.

Henri's evil army kept advancing. A puppet's head lurched

sideways atop its neck. A doll's button eye dangled on a dirty string.

Belle grabbed a candlestick off the desk and used it to smash one of the glass panes. She reached through the broken glass and tried to turn the handle from the outside, but it still wouldn't move.

The creatures were only yards away now. Belle turned in a frantic circle, desperate to find a way out, a way to save herself and her friends.

Her eyes fell on a chair. It was pushed under the desk. She pulled it out.

"Belle, get out of there! They're coming straight for you!" Lucanos shouted.

Belle dragged the heavy chair over to the French doors.

"Time to start writing my own story, Lucanos," she said.

Using all the strength she possessed, Belle hoisted the chair over her head. And then, with an ear-splitting yell, she launched it straight at the French doors.

CHAPTER FIFTY-SEVEN

GLASS SHATTERED AND WOOD SPLIT as the heavy chair burst through the doors.

It left a gaping hole in its wake.

"Let's go!" Lucanos urged, swooping down from the ceiling. He was outside in an instant.

Aranae was right behind him. Belle ran back to Otto.

"Leave me, Belle," he said. "I'll only slow you down."

But Belle didn't listen to him. She gently raised the lower half of his leg, meaning to rotate it, but the movement caused him to lose his balance. He pitched forward into the desk.

The shambling conglomeration of puppets and dolls was

closing in. Some were upright, others slumped—their sad, empty eyes staring straight ahead.

Belle knew she had only seconds. She twisted the bottom of Otto's leg roughly, then jammed the metal ball joint of his knee back into its socket.

Otto gasped.

"Come on!" Belle shouted, grabbing his hand.

She shot through the doorway, pulling him after her. They made it out by a hair's breadth.

Lucanos and Aranae were waiting for them. "Let's *go!*" the beetle said.

"That was exciting!" Otto said.

"Yes, Otto, it was. A little *too* exciting," Belle said. "How's your leg?" she asked him.

"It's fine!" he said, shaking it. "See?"

"Good. We've got to hurry. Can you run?"

"I'll try," Otto said gamely. "I love running! And escaping—I *love* escaping!"

"I am going to kill him before this is over. Or myself," Lucanos declared.

"I know what we're running from," Otto said, "But what are we running *to?*"

"To the château. To find the countess," Belle replied, with

a new determination in her voice. "She doesn't get to tell my story. *I do.*"

Belle checked that she still had her handkerchief and her coin, then ran down the drive toward the dirt road that led back to the château, with Otto rattling along beside her, Aranae hanging on to her shoulder for dear life, and Lucanos flying right behind them.

CHAPTER FIFTY-EIGHT

"THIS WAY! HURRY!" Chip shouted, zooming down the long row of bookcases.

The Beast was right behind him, along with Lumiere, Mrs. Potts, Cogsworth, Plumette, and Froufrou.

Chip raced to the end of the row, turned, and dashed to a door between two bookcases. It was slightly ajar.

"I had no idea there was another room back here!" Lumiere said.

"It was a workroom," the Beast explained. "For the castle's librarian."

The Beast cautiously entered. His servants followed him.

He immediately saw that Belle was not in the room—but something else was.

Near the window, an enormous book stood open, its pages showing a picture of an overgrown garden. The picture looked as if it were behind thick glass.

The Beast's hackles rose as he looked at it. A menacing growl escaped from his throat. He knew that the library contained enchantment, but his instincts told him that this one was new and different, that it was a dark, malevolent thing.

"What is it, master?" Mrs. Potts asked.

"It's a magical book, but one I haven't seen before. I'm not sure what it does."

"Stand back, everyone!" Cogsworth declared. He grabbed a measuring stick that was leaning against a wall and thrust it at the book.

It made a sharp sound as it hit the page, as if it had struck ice.

"Belle's in there," Chip said.

"How do you know that, Chip?" Lumiere asked.

Chip pointed at the floor with his handle. Lying on it, just in front of the book, was a blue ribbon—Belle's ribbon.

"She left us. She's *gone*," said Chip.

The Beast knew what the heaviness in the youngster's

voice meant. By losing Belle, the servants had lost their one and only chance at breaking the curse that had changed them into what they now were, that had bound them to this castle, this life, this fate . . . forever.

Mrs. Potts turned away from the book, but not before the Beast heard a small sob escape her.

He knew she wasn't thinking of herself, or him, or any of the servants. She was thinking of one person only—Chip, her little boy. She was thinking of how his life would now end here, in this cursed castle, before it had even begun.

Cogsworth put the measuring stick back where'd he gotten it, silent for once.

Lumiere, his flames dimmed, traded heartbroken glances with Plumette.

The Beast picked up the blue ribbon and turned away from the others, his head bowed, his heart as heavy as stone.

CHAPTER FIFTY-NINE

"LEFT OR RIGHT?" Lucanos shouted as they neared the dirt road at the end of the driveway.

"Left!" a breathless Belle shouted back.

She ran full speed into the road, Aranae still clinging to her shoulder, then glanced behind her to make sure Lucanos and Otto were still there.

Lucanos was, but Otto wasn't.

"Otto! Where are you?" she called, doubling back.

She soon had her answer.

He was lying on the ground at the edge of the road, looking dazed.

"What are you doing?" she asked, helping him up. "This is no time for fooling. We have a long way to go!"

"I—I fell," he said, pushing himself off the ground. He walked shakily toward the road, but as he tried to walk into it, he bounced backward and crashed to the ground again.

It was as if he'd walked into a wall.

"What's going on?" Belle wondered aloud. She took his hand. "We'll walk through together," she said, pulling him after her. But it didn't help. She could walk into the road, but he couldn't.

Lucanos, who'd been flying around in circles, landed on Belle's other shoulder. "It's the countess's work," he said grimly. "She's bound him to this place."

Otto nodded. "He's right. That's why all the other marionettes and mannequins in the summer house aren't wandering away from it. You have to go on without me," he said.

"No," said Belle. "There must be a way to get you out of here."

"There isn't," Otto said. "And you're losing time. You have to go. *Now*, Belle."

"But what will happen to you?" Belle asked. "What if the countess finds out that you helped us? What if she punishes you?"

"She can't punish me if she can't wind me," said Otto. "Take the key out of my back and throw it away. Toss it into a pond. Down a well. Someplace she'll never find it."

"But that . . . that means . . . the end of you," Belle said softly.

"It's all right, Belle," Otto said, smiling bravely. "I'm quite sure that I've lived, and loved, more in one hour than many humans do in a lifetime."

Belle put her arms around him and hugged him tightly.

Otto hugged her back. "Before you go, promise me something, Belle . . ." he whispered to her. "Keep being the author of your own story. Never let anyone else write it for you again."

"I promise," Belle said, in a small, choked voice.

Otto held her tightly for a few more seconds, then released her. His smiled faded. His gaze turned inward. He clutched his red silk heart.

"Otto? What's wrong?"

He looked at her, confusion in his eyes. "Oh, my. Oh, dear," he said. "Is this also love? This terrible pain?"

Belle nodded.

"Love is hard. I had no idea how hard. Is it worth the pain?"

"Yes," Belle said. "It is."

"Please, Belle," Otto said. "If I have to go, I want to go with my friends around me . . . with love. . . ."

Belle steeled herself. Then she grasped the key and pulled it out. The light went out of Otto's glass eyes. His smiled dimmed. He slumped over.

Belle pressed a hand to her own heart now. It hurt terribly.

She remembered the words of her friend Agathe. *Love is not for cowards,* she had said.

"You were the bravest, Otto," she whispered.

"The château is half an hour from the summer house by coach, and you're on foot. We *must* get going," Lucanos said. He was still sitting on her shoulder.

Belle nodded. "Then let's go."

Lucanos flew off ahead of her.

But not before Belle saw a shimmer of tears in the beetle's bright black eyes.

CHAPTER SIXTY

BELLE, SO EXHAUSTED she could barely walk, leaned against a tree near the countess's château to catch her breath.

Her dress was covered with dust from the dirt road. Its hem was torn from thorns and brambles, and wet from dragging along the edge of a weed-choked pond where she'd stopped to throw away Otto's key.

It had taken her over two hours to walk from the summer house to the château because the road was now densely overgrown. In places, she'd had to fight her way through branches and step over thick tangles of vines.

The extent of the countess's enchantment became apparent to Belle as she walked along. What she'd thought were lush pear, apple, or cherry orchards actually contained spindly black trees bearing pomegranates. Large, tumbledown stone barns had been made to look like the Palais-Royal, with pillars propped up in front of them and half-rotted wagons standing in as carriages. The ride she and the countess had supposedly taken from the château to Paris, Belle now realized, had probably carried them no farther than this very dirt road.

Lucanos, tired himself, was resting on Belle's upturned palm. "I can barely *see* the château," he said.

The trees that lined the graveled drive had grown so tall, and their branches had knotted so closely together, that they obscured it.

After she'd rested for a moment, Belle made her way up the drive. It was dark now. The moon was behind a cloud, but it still gave off enough light to illuminate her way.

As she neared the château, she saw that many of its windows were broken. A hole gaped in the roof. Moss had crept over the two stone lions that flanked the crumbling, once-elegant staircase.

Belle stopped when she reached the steps and looked up at the house. She saw the ghostly glow of a candelabrum moving past the windows.

"She's here," she said grimly.

Then she started up the steps.

CHAPTER SIXTY-ONE

BELLE STOOD IN FRONT of the door to the countess's dwelling and grasped its immense bronze handle.

She felt as if the task ahead of her was all but impossible. She and Lucanos had tried to come up with a plan as they'd made their way here, but had discovered that it was difficult to make a plan when you had no idea what you were planning for.

"How are we going to do this?" Lucanos asked now, his voice a whisper. "How do we get the bracelet?"

"Ask the countess for it politely?" Belle offered, with a mirthless laugh.

She pushed on the door. The hinges moaned softly as it

opened; Belle desperately hoped that no one else had heard them.

She crept across the foyer now, listening for voices or movement. Someone had been walking through the house with a candelabrum only moments ago. Who was it?

An instant later, she had her answer.

Mouchard, in human form once again, came bustling into view, heavily laden. Trotting along behind him was another servant, a young woman.

A wide stone staircase spiraled up from the foyer to the upper floors. Belle, Lucanos, and Aranae had just enough time to crouch down in the hollow under it.

"Her Ladyship has retired for the evening," Mouchard said, stopping only a few feet away from Belle and her friends. "She's not to be disturbed. Tell the other servants to stay off the third floor." He piled the heap of clothing he was carrying into the maid's arms and continued.

"Clean the comtesse's traveling cloak, polish her boots, and shine her walking stick. Have them ready by morning," he instructed. "A fever has broken out in Venice. She wishes to depart at dawn."

The maid gave a curt nod and scurried off in one direction. Mouchard continued in another.

"I know what to do!" Belle whispered excitedly as soon as they were gone.

"Well, dear girl, don't keep it to yourself," Lucanos said.

"The countess is asleep. She's bound to have taken her jewelry off and put it down somewhere—on a table or in a jewelry box. All we have to do is sneak into her room and take it!"

"What a wonderful plan!" Lucanos said. "All we have to do is rob Death herself. Nothing to it!"

Belle gave him a sidelong look. "Do you have a better idea?"

"Unfortunately, no," said Lucanos.

"Come on, let's go," said Belle, stepping out from her hiding place. "We know where her room is, thanks to Mouchard."

The three crept up the stairs silently. When they reached the third-floor landing, they saw that a wide corridor led off in two directions. The eastern half lay in darkness. Candles burned in wall sconces in the western half. More candlelight was shining out from under a door at the corridor's end.

Lucanos pointed at it. "Something tells me that's her room," he said.

Belle, Lucanos, and Aranae quietly approached the door. Belle put her ear against it but heard nothing. She grasped the knob and turned it.

Light flooded her eyes as the door swung open. Pillar candles, at least a hundred of them, were burning in the room.

A heavy, spicy scent filled the air. Belle recognized it as the countess's perfume. But she'd smelled it elsewhere, too, and now she realized where—at funerals held in Villeneuve's church. Myrrh, oils of cinnamon and clove—these things were used to anoint the dead.

The thought unnerved her. It reminded her, as if she needed any reminding, of just whom she was dealing with.

The room was cold and sparsely furnished, its ceiling high and peaked. The countess reclined on a massive four-poster bed. Its pillars had been carved to resemble skeletons. On its headboard another skeleton was carved, this one sitting on a throne and wearing a laurel wreath on its skull. It reminded Belle of a tombstone.

The countess's eyes were closed. Her right hand rested on her chest; her left was at her side. Belle's heart sank as she saw that the countess hadn't taken the bracelet off. It was still wound around her wrist. How would they remove it without waking her?

"This just got a lot harder," she whispered.

She moved toward the bed, but Aranae held up one of her long legs, stopping her.

Noiselessly, the spider scuttled up the headboard, positioned herself at the top of it, and started to spin, tossing her sticky, silken thread over the countess.

Clever spider! Belle thought.

Quickly and diligently Aranae worked, careful not to cover either the bracelet or the countess's face, lest the countess feel the threads on her skin and wake. A quarter of an hour later, her body was blanketed in white spider silk and bound to the bedframe.

"Thank you, Aranae!" Belle whispered as the spider climbed down.

Aranae nodded. Belle crept toward the sleeping figure. Her heart was pounding. She had to squeeze her hands into fists to keep them from shaking.

When she reached the bed, she took a deep breath. Then she bent over the countess and carefully released the catch on the bracelet's gold clasp.

The clasp snapped open.

And so did the countess's eyes.

CHAPTER SIXTY-TWO

"YOU."

The countess spoke the word coolly. She tried to get up, but couldn't. She looked calmly down the length of her body; then her eyes found Belle's again.

"There are a thousand ways to die, my dear," she said. "Some are easy, and others are very, very hard. Yours will be in the latter category if you take the bracelet from me."

Gulping with terror, Belle quickly unwound the bracelet from the countess's wrist.

Then she ran for her life.

CHAPTER SIXTY-THREE

OUT OF THE COUNTESS'S BEDROOM, through the long corridor, and down the spiraling staircase Belle flew, with Lucanos and Aranae leading the way.

Just as she got to the bottom of the stairs, Mouchard—drawn by the noisy echo of Belle's boots on the steps—came hurrying into the foyer. He squawked with anger as he saw Belle, then charged at her.

She had no hope of ducking by him; he was too large and too fast. She looked around wildly, not knowing which way to run. Then Lucanos, who was on the floor between Belle and Mouchard, yelled, "The bracelet, Belle! Throw it to me!"

Belle did. The beetle caught it. He held onto one end and tossed the other to Aranae. Pulling it tight between them, they tripped the charging Mouchard. He went sprawling and hit the stone floor with a shuddering thud.

"Run, Belle, *run!*" Lucanos shouted, lobbing the bracelet back to her.

Belle caught it and raced out the door. She flew down the steps and headed for the drive. But it was gone. Rosebushes had completely overgrown it.

Belle hurried through them, trying her best to navigate toward the portal. Thorns as long as her thumb jutted from the rosebushes' shaggy canes. The roses themselves had grown as large as dinner plates. Their petaled faces followed Belle as she ran by. She was sure she heard them whispering to each other.

As soon as she was through the roses, Belle was confronted by another obstacle—a solid wall of green. The yew trees had formed themselves into a maze. Branches, densely grown together, blocked her way. Narrow paths snaked off to her left and right.

"Which way?" Lucanos asked.

"I don't know," Belle said. She would have to guess and hope for the best. "Head to the right," she said.

The three hurried along, moonbeams lighting their way. Moments later, the pathway pinwheeled to a dead end.

"Crumbs!" Belle said frantically. She turned around, ready to retrace her steps, and gasped.

A toad blocked her path. Belle had seen him once before, but he'd been only as big as a cat then. He was the size of a pony now. His gold eyes appraised her, then swiveled to Lucanos and Aranae. A thick string of silvery drool dripped from the corner of his enormous mouth.

Aranae chittered fearfully.

"Yes, I *see* that it's a toad. And yes, I *know* what toads eat!" Lucanos said nervously.

The toad shuffled toward them on his stumpy legs. His giant white belly dragged on the ground.

"Don't even think about it," Belle cautioned, pushing Lucanos and Aranae behind her.

But the toad kept coming.

Thinking fast, Belle broke off a branch from a yew tree.

"Last warning," she said, waving the stick.

But the greedy toad paid her no attention, so Belle whacked him across his snout. The creature squealed in pain, then burrowed under some low branches.

Belle struggled on. Night birds called out, their songs

sinister and harsh. Creatures slithered and scuttled underfoot.

She and her friends went down one new pathway, then another, trying to get to the middle of the maze, but again and again they found only dead ends.

After yet another fruitless try, Belle—her hands and arms scratched from the thorns, sticks and leaves in her hair—stopped, desperate to get her bearings. Panic started to whisper in her ear, telling her that she would never get out of the maze. But she refused to give in to it; she knew that if she did, she would be truly lost.

She started walking again and had just found a new pathway to try when she heard it—a low, deep sound, like millstones grinding. Or like someone pushing open the heavy stone door of a tomb.

"What is that?" Lucanos asked. "It almost sounds like growling."

The noise came again. It was closer this time. So close it seemed to be on the other side of the hedge wall.

Belle's blood ran cold. "Aranae, Lucanos . . . run," she said, her voice barely a whisper. "Run!"

"Run? Why?" Lucanos asked. "What's going—"

The beetle's words were cut off as Belle snatched him up. There was no time to explain. She grabbed Aranae, too, then shot down the new pathway she'd found, praying it was the right one.

The noises they'd heard could have only one source, and Belle knew what it was.

The countess's stone lions.

CHAPTER SIXTY-FOUR

STUMBLING AND TRIPPING, Belle ran down the path. Her dress caught on a branch. She tore it free.

"What's going on?" Lucanos demanded. "Unhand me this instant!"

"Lions . . ." Belle panted. "The statues . . . from the staircase . . ."

A roar ripped through the night. It was followed by a second one. They seemed to be coming from two different directions now.

"They've split up," Belle said. "They're stalking us."

She turned a corner and continued down the path, following it as it snaked off farther into the maze.

Where's the portal? she wondered frantically. *Maybe at that next corner up ahead. We must be getting close.*

She was halfway to the corner when a creature rounded it from the opposite direction.

Belle froze.

Carved of white marble, the lion glowed in the moonlight. A lush mane flowed down its neck to its powerful shoulders. Muscles rippled under its fur with every step it took. An eerie blue light flickered in its eyes.

As those eyes found Belle, the lion snarled, revealing a set of sharp, pointed fangs.

Slowly, Belle backed away. She glanced behind her, and as she did, the second lion appeared at the other end of the row, blocking her escape.

Heads down, tails lashing, they closed in. There was nowhere for Belle to go.

"No," she said, her eyes wide with fear. "Please . . . *no!*"

Her legs started to shake.

"There's no way out, Belle. It's over," Lucanos said brokenly.

"No, Lucanos. I won't let her do this. There's *always* a way. If I can't go left or right, then I've got to go up!" Belle said resolutely.

She faced the hedge, grabbed a branch, and started to

climb. Aranae scuttled up ahead of her. Lucanos flew.

When the lions realized what the three were doing, they broke into a run.

"Hurry, Belle. *Faster!*" Lucanos shouted.

He flew underneath her and poked her in the rump with his sharp horns, again and again.

"Ouch!" Belle yelped, scrambling higher.

The yew's branches were dense. They slapped at Belle's cheeks and poked her eyes. The bark scraped her skin. She ignored the pain and kept going. In only a few seconds, she was a good ten feet off the ground.

The lions circled below her and roared. One started to scale the yew. Like most lions, it was a good climber—but unlike most lions, it was made of stone, and the yew's branches snapped like matchsticks under its weight.

Higher and higher Belle climbed. Now almost at the top of the trees, she was just about to put her right foot on a sturdy branch when the limb beneath her left foot broke.

Belle screamed. Her hands tightened around the branches they were holding. Her legs dangled over the path. The lions jumped as high as they could, swiping at her feet with their lethal claws, but they couldn't reach her.

After what seemed like an eternity, Belle managed to plant

her right foot on a branch. Then her left foot. She resumed her climb, and a moment later, reached the top of the tree line.

She looked over the edge to the other side, and let out a long, loud whoop of relief.

Below her was the book. And with it, the way out of *Nevermore.*

She was almost home.

CHAPTER SIXTY-FIVE

"ALMOST THERE. KEEP GOING. One step at a time," Belle said to herself.

She was most of the way down the other side of the yew hedge, and almost out of the maze. Glancing over her shoulder, she saw the book, right where it should be. In only seconds, she'd be walking through it, leaving *Nevermore* and the countess behind her.

She jumped the last few feet, landing with a whump on the ground.

"Thank you, Lucanos. Thank you, Aranae!" she said to her friends, who were already down. "I think we're going to make it."

But Lucanos didn't reply. His eyes were on *Nevermore*.

Belle followed his gaze and saw that the silvery shimmer of its surface wasn't rippling as it usually did. It wasn't moving at all. It was perfectly still, glassed over like a winter lake.

Belle pressed her palm against it. It was as hard and as cold as ice. She looked through it, expecting to see the workroom and the table and desk inside it.

Instead she saw the Beast. He was holding a blue ribbon in his paw—*her* blue ribbon. He was looking into the pages of *Nevermore*.

Belle could see him and the others because the workroom was illuminated by candles. On this side of the book, however, there was only darkness; they could not see her.

She stared at the Beast, quizzically. She would have expected him to roar and rage, to lash out and smash something.

Instead, he looked heartbroken.

And as she gazed at his face, Belle saw something she hadn't seen before—that the Beast truly cared for her.

"Someone stole her!" Cogsworth declared. "We must arm ourselves, master! We must go after the rogue who committed this foul deed and bring Belle back!"

The Beast slowly shook his head. "You don't understand, Cogsworth. No one took Belle—she left. Because she wanted to. I'd go in if I could, but it's impossible. Belle made a choice, and it was hers and hers alone."

The Beast looked devastated as he said these words. Belle's eyes traveled to Cogsworth's face, then Lumiere's, Mrs. Potts's, Plumette's. They *all* looked devastated.

A small sniffle was heard. Then another.

It was Chip.

"No!" Belle whispered. "Please, Chip . . . please don't cry!"

"Why did Belle want to leave, Mama? Was she so unhappy with us?" he asked.

Mrs. Potts, infinitely gentle with her young son, said, "Hush, my darling. We mustn't cry for ourselves."

"I'm not. I'm crying for Belle. Because her heart was hurting."

Belle leaned her forehead against the cold page. Her heart was doing more than hurting; it was breaking.

She felt terrible—because she'd hurt Chip and all the others, but also because Chip was right.

"I was unhappy. I *did* want to leave," she whispered. "And now all I want is to be back with you."

The Beast gently laid her blue ribbon on the desk. Watching him do it was like a knife to her heart. It felt final. Irrevocable. Like throwing a handful of dirt on a coffin.

Belle wished she'd never laid eyes on *Nevermore*. She remembered how excited she'd been when she first discovered it, when she'd first stepped through its pages. The girl who had ventured into that book had fallen for an easy escape. She'd believed that a pretty, perfect, unreal world was preferable to the hard, messy, real one.

"But it's not," she said now.

She missed the real world desperately, even with all of its difficulties. And she missed the ones who lived in it. As her gaze traveled over the faces on the other side, she realized that it wasn't only a person's strengths but their flaws, that made them truly beautiful.

What would Chip be without his chip? The chunk missing from his rim only made him sweeter. And Cogsworth? His constant fretting and hand-wringing could be so irritating at times, but it was only his blustery way of showing concern for those he loved.

And the Beast . . . the *Beast*.

Belle saw now that his gruff, sometimes-frightening exterior masked a kind and loyal heart. He would give his life to save her if he could.

"Beast," she whispered.

As if he'd heard her, he walked up to *Nevermore*. His eyes traveled over it, searching—Belle knew—for a glimpse of her. He pressed a paw against its hard surface. Belle fit her hand to its outline.

"Beast," she cried. "Oh, *Beast*."

She wanted to be with him—with all of them. But it was too late. She'd gotten the bracelet, the handkerchief, and the coin back, but it was all for nothing. The passageway between the Beast's castle and *Nevermore* was sealed.

Desperate, Belle slapped her hands against the pages. As she did, she realized that her skin was almost completely covered with words.

"No!" she cried. Her time was almost up.

She slapped the page again, trying one last time to make the Beast see her.

"Save your breath, my dear. He can't see or hear you," said a voice from behind her.

Belle's stomach plunged with fear. She slowly turned around.

And faced the countess.

CHAPTER SIXTY-SIX

STICKY SKEINS OF SPIDER SILK hung from the countess's black gown. Moonlight glimmered in her cold, green eyes. She and her lions had come out of the maze, too. They were a good ten yards away, but getting closer with every step.

"This game grows tiresome," the countess said. She thrust out a pale hand, her nails curved like claws. "Give me the bracelet, the handkerchief, and the coin. *Now.*"

Belle shook her head.

The countess laughed. It sounded like wind whistling through a graveyard. A shutter banging. Footsteps in the dark.

"My dear, you do *not* want to make me any angrier than I already am. Trust me on that."

Belle turned and threw herself at *Nevermore* with all her might. "Mrs. Potts! Lumiere!" she shouted. "Help! It's me, Belle!"

She hammered on the page with her fists, slapped it with her palms. And all the while, the countess moved closer.

"Because of you, this game was trickier than I thought it would be," she said. "And yet, what fun is any game without a challenge? I can't wait to see my sister's face when I tell her I won."

"Cogsworth, *please!* Can't you see me?"

A movement on her right side caught Belle's eye. She turned her head, fearing it was the countess, but it was Lucanos, circling madly.

"Use your *heart*, Belle!" he shouted.

What did he mean? The countess was only steps away. How would Belle's *heart* help defeat her?

"Your heart, Belle!" the beetle shouted again. "Your *heart!*"

The beetle was close now, and pointing frantically at her chest. Belle looked down and caught her breath. The glass heart, the one the Beast had given her, looked as if it were ablaze. Now that Belle was out of the shadowy maze, moonbeams were shining down directly on the heart, refracting into a million points of light.

Astonished, Belle saw that it wasn't plain glass as she'd thought, or even fine crystal, but diamond.

Belle knew that there was nothing harder. She remembered that her father used a diamond-tipped tool to cut tiny windows for his music boxes from sheets of glass.

Belle yanked the jewel from her neck. Using the heart like a blade, she drew it down the length of *Nevermore's* page and opened a long, rippling gash.

As she did, she heard a shriek of fury. She knew without looking that the countess was only a few yards behind her.

She turned. "Lucanos . . . Aranae . . ." she said, with a choked cry.

"*Go!*" Lucanos bellowed.

"Thank you . . . *thank you,*" Belle said.

The countess lunged, her clawed hand outstretched, but her fingers closed on air.

Belle was gone.

CHAPTER SIXTY-SEVEN

STARS WERE THE FIRST thing Belle saw.

They exploded like fireworks behind her eyes.

Then she saw feathers. The base of a teapot. Golden feet. Furry feet.

I'm here! she thought. *I'm home!*

Belle had launched herself back through *Nevermore* with such force, she'd lost her footing and tumbled headfirst into the library. She was lying facedown on the floor now, grateful for the plush rug.

"Belle!" a voice cried. Others joined in.

"You came back!"

"We were so worried!"

She felt the Beast's paws helping her up. As she stood on her feet again, her eyes fell on *Nevermore*, standing open in the room.

"Close it! Please!" she begged, fearing the countess would come through it after her.

"We will, Belle. Don't worry," Lumiere said, hurrying to the book. He pushed against the cover, and it swung shut with a bang. The book began to shrink.

Belle looked at her hands. The print that had covered them was gone.

A ragged sigh of relief escaped her. "I'm here! I'm alive!" she said. She turned to Lumiere and hugged him. "I thought I'd never see you again!"

She hugged Cogsworth, too, and Mrs. Potts and Plumette. She picked up little Chip and kissed him, then patted Froufrou.

"Where's . . ." she started to ask, looking for the Beast.

She spotted him standing in a corner of the room, hanging back, uncertain.

Belle took a step toward him, then another, and then threw her arms around him and buried her face in his neck. "I couldn't get back here. I tried and tried," she said, her voice catching. "Your heart . . . the one you gave me . . . that's how I finally got out. It saved me. Without it, without you . . . I never would have made it."

"Shh, Belle. It's all right. You found your way. That's all that matters," the Beast whispered, holding her tightly.

Belle nodded. After a moment, when she'd hugged him hard enough and long enough to convince herself that he was real, she released him.

Seeing tears on her cheeks, the Beast wiped them away with the back of his furry paw.

"Oh!" Belle said, wincing. It was like having her cheeks scrubbed with a shoe brush.

"Ahem."

It was Lumiere. "If I may . . ." He was holding out a handkerchief.

Belle took it from him and patted her cheeks dry.

"I think a nice pot of tea and a plate of toasted cheese sandwiches are precisely what's required. I'll bring them to the drawing room. Cogsworth will arrange for a lovely fire for you there. Won't you, Cogsworth?"

"Now, I don't see what all the kerfuffle is about. She's back and clearly—" Cogsworth began.

Mrs. Potts glared.

"I mean, *I will!* Right away."

The servants hurried out of the library, leaving the Beast and Belle alone.

"Goodness me!" whispered Mrs. Potts as soon as they were out of the Beast's earshot. "Wiping the poor girl's face with the back of his paw . . . I mean, *really!*" She sighed. "I despair sometimes. Are we *ever* going to civilize our master?"

"At least he didn't lick her face. That's something," Plumette whispered back, giggling.

"Let's hope he doesn't carry her to the drawing room by the scruff of her neck!" Mrs. Potts added, laughing herself now.

"There's hope," Lumiere said, his flames brightening. "For Belle. For the master. For all of us."

"There's *always* hope," said Cogsworth sagely. "Why, did I ever tell you about the time Prince Ferdinand of Brunswick tried to drive the maréchal de Broglie out of Westphalia? It was during the battle of Bergen. Things looked dire indeed. The Hessians had us surrounded. . . ."

Mrs. Potts and Plumette traded exasperated glances, then hurried down the stairs as fast as they could. Chip, Froufrou, and Lumiere followed them. Cogsworth, seemingly unaware that his audience had disappeared, continued to hold forth.

Back in the library, Belle cupped her elbows. She was trying to work up her courage.

"Shall we go to the drawing room? Or do you not want toasted cheese sandwiches?" the Beast asked Belle.

"I can't even tell you how badly I want them," Belle replied. "But there's something I need to do first."

Nevermore had shrunk down to its normal size. Though Belle was afraid of it, she made herself pick it up. Then she crossed the room, to the passage leading into the library, and opened one of the windows along the hall. A brisk, icy wind swirled in.

She held the book for a long moment, her head bent. She silently thanked Lucanos and Aranae, wherever they might be. She promised Otto that she would never forget him. And she remembered the comtesse des Terres des Morts, shivering at how close she'd come to letting that dark figure finish her story before it had even begun.

Then, Belle flung the book out of the window. The wind pounced. It grabbed *Nevermore*, tore its pages loose, and carried them away.

Belle slammed the window shut and turned around. Her chest was heaving. Her cheeks were pink from the wind. Her hair was wild.

The Beast pulled her blue ribbon from his breast pocket. He handed it to her.

"Thank you," she said, taking it. She tried to tie her hair back with it, but her hands were shaking so badly, she couldn't.

The Beast noticed. His eyes, worried but warm and kind, sought hers. "Do you want to tell me about it?" he asked, taking her hands to steady them.

"It's such a strange tale, I'm not sure you'd believe me."

The Beast laughed. "I just might. I have some acquaintance with strange things, you know."

Belle gave him a rueful smile. She looked down at her hands in his paws.

"Belle? What's wrong?" the Beast asked.

"It doesn't always go so well when you and I try to talk, does it?"

The Beast shook his head. "No, it doesn't," he admitted. "I'm not much of a communicator. In fact, I don't have much practice in being a perfect friend. Or a friend at all, really."

Belle thought about her "perfect" friends within Nevermore. The countess and her dazzling guests. Mouchard. Professore Truffatore, Henri.

"Neither do I. You may not be a 'perfect friend,'" she said. "But you're a real one. And I'm lucky to have you."

337

The Beast smiled. He squeezed her hands. "Can we keep trying, Belle? Would you give me another chance?"

Belle smiled.

She squeezed back.

And decided that she would.

EPILOGUE

IN THE HOLLOW TRUNK of an ancient willow tree, near a clear, rushing stream, Love and Death played their eternal game.

Love was mistress of the willow, and any mortal who sat down beneath its softly sighing branches, no matter how weary or without hope, found his heart full and his spirit restored.

She and Death sat in chairs woven of branches. A large speckled toadstool served as their table. Fireflies hovered in the air above them, illuminating the deep night.

Their chessboard was made of obsidian and bone. Insects were the chess pieces.

"It's your move," Death said, drumming her fingers on the arm of her chair.

"Yes, I know," said Love.

"We don't have all night," said Death.

"You can't hurry love," said Love.

A moment later, her queen—a praying mantis—ate one of Death's pawns—a plump yellow caterpillar.

"How was your trip to Venice?" Love asked as Death contemplated the board.

"Productive. The outbreak was rather severe, I'm happy to say," Death replied. "Ten thousand gone in a week—a personal best. I brought you some candy."

Love smiled. "Did you bring me three million louis d'or?"

"No," replied Death. "Why would I? You haven't won the wager."

"I'm going to, though," said Love confidently.

Death frowned. She nudged her knight—a grasshopper—forward. It bit the head off Love's rook—a moth.

"I *always* win," said Love.

Death sat back in her chair and regarded her sister. "Has anyone ever told you that it's rude to brag?"

"The Beast is learning to care for others," Love said. "His heart aches over what he's done. He's learning to love. Belle is teaching him. He would die for that girl."

"Would he?" Death asked. "I'd be happy to arrange it."

Love ignored the dark jest. "The Beast will love, and be

loved in return, before the last petal on the enchanted rose falls. Wait and see."

Death shook her head. "Once again, you fail to see the bigger question: Will Belle learn to love the Beast?"

"She will. She *is*. They're becoming friends. That's the first step."

"Don't be so certain. The story's not over. Much can still go wrong," said Death. "And if the human heart is involved, much will."

"I'm hopeful," said Love.

"Fools always are," sighed Death. She nodded at the board. "It's your move."

Love turned her attention back to the chessboard, determination etched on her face. Death sat forward, her brow knit in concentration.

Attacks and counterattacks, binds and blockades, feints and ripostes followed as the sisters vied to win.

Beneath the canopy of night, into the clear light of morning, the brightness of daytime, and the softly falling dusk, the hours passed.

From long, long ago to forevermore, Love and Death played on.